I0645476

A Woman Apart

Lai Tan

Copyright © 2022 *Lai Tan*

All Rights Reserved

Dedication

To Emmanuel, TT, Adam and Zara.

About The Author

Lai Tan was born in Ibadan, the third largest city in Nigeria. She comes from a large family of seven children.

Lai always has a story writing itself inside her head and draws inspiration from events around her. She was that child and then the teenager who wrote happy endings whilst surrounded by life's hardships.

She partly lives in the real world and a fantasy one. She has completed several manuscripts over the years but has not ventured into the world of romance publishing until now.

Lai lives in Greater Manchester, United Kingdom, with her partner and three kids. She is a hopeless romantic who enjoys the thrills that come with manipulating a more pleasant world on the inside than the reality we all live on the outside.

She considers the biggest compliments paid to her writing as being asked if she was a writer, off sending people one or two lines in a text message!

Chapter One

Sade knocked hesitantly on the principal's door. This was a meeting she did not see the need for. She had a pretty good idea what this summons was for. But surely, the principal stepping into it was a matter of the mountain and the molehill. Mr Korede, the history teacher, had told her Principal Davies wanted to see her immediately after another one of his lectures on the Oyo Empire. Today had been about the despicable Bashorun Gaa. The history of the empire was written in wars, murder, suicide, patricide, and all manners of ways man was cruel to fellow man. Violence was woven, she had since decided, in the fabric of man. Israel and Palestine were still at it.

"Come on in." The principal called from the other side of the door.

Sade stepped into the room. It was not her first time. It was a large airy room with soft plush dark green carpeting. Principal Davies, as always, sat behind an enormous mahogany desk, on top of which were several files of varied thickness, a desktop computer, a vase with artificial orchids, and a tabletop photo frame of the principal's family of four. The wall behind the principal hosted framed pictures of the Nigerian president, the senate president, the state governor, and Principal Davies.

"Good afternoon, madam," Sade said warily as she was waved to the straight back chair across from the principal. Sade sat down.

The principal was a plump, bespectacled woman in her early fifties with a reputation for not suffering fools gladly. She went straight to the point.

"I have called you here because of things I have heard from the grapevine."

The legendary grapevine was a group of girls, allegedly sworn to secrecy by the principal, who informed Davies of who was up to no good among the girls. No one seemed to know these snitches, but the principal claimed they existed. There were rumours among the girls about the traitors in their midst, but no one had been able to prove anything yet. Sade herself had been accused on a couple of occasions. She was beginning to think the grapevine was a myth.

"About what?" Sade kept a solemn face. She was not about to give away anything if the principal had little to go on.

"The Fernandez interview," Davies said bluntly, her stern expression warning Sade not to patronise her.

"Anne is doing it." Sade blurted out. She took a deep breath and said more slowly. "Anne is happy to do it."

"So will many girls, I gather," Principal Davies noted, tapping her left middle finger on the big desk. "Why did you choose Anne? Because she is your best friend?"

Sade shook her head. "No. She is terrific, and if she wasn't adamant about being a nun, I'm sure she'd make an excellent journalist."

"Is that why you picked her? Because she said she is going to be a nun?"

Partly true that. But Sade said nothing. Principal Davies looked down at the desk, trying very hard not to laugh. Oh, the naivety of youth!

"You know, Sade, what people say they will do and what they do, are not necessarily the same thing,"

Davies said in a softer tone. "I know it is your job as the editor to assign tasks in the press club, and I try not to barrel into these student affairs."

No kidding.

"But when a celebrity pop singer like Mayowa Fernandez is dropping into our lit evening, and my girls start threatening to kill each other over who interviews him for the Term magazine, I feel the need to step in. Plus, Mayowa does not exactly have the reputation of a saint. He will not be allowed to bring disrepute to this school."

Sade sighed. No one was killing anybody. Yes, it was true that a few threats had been thrown here and there by some other members of the club. Sade had intentionally kept the identity of the selected interviewer secret until now. She had planned to let it on, on the day when it would be too late for anyone to do anything about it. Her position as the school press club editor was one of the most coveted and competed for in the school. Sade even had a tiny office in the English block where she wrote and reviewed articles and press releases. Quietly. Being the head girl was the next best thing. But who needed all that attention?

"No one else knows it's Anne. We've managed to keep it secret, which is why you've not heard about it from your grapevine. She can't be threatened if they don't know she is doing it." Sade said lightly.

"I do agree it is a smart move to keep it secret. But I am not convinced about Anne. Anne has the making of a good writer. However, she also strikes me as someone impressionable. I want someone not easily overwhelmed, someone unlikely to get star-struck. Someone who doesn't give a hoot. And yet will do an excellent job of the interview itself. Someone like you."

Sade stared at her disbelievingly. She did not just hear that.

"You want me to interview Mayowa Fernandez?"

"Why not? The very fact that you asked someone else to do it tells me you are the least interested in meeting him, and that makes you, in my eyes, the perfect one for the job."

Ask someone else to do it? It was called delegation. Oh no, she was not interested in standing within a few metres of a man who probably thought he was God's gift to the world. She could not stand the ilk!

She took another deep breath and said dispassionately, "I really am not the perfect one. If Mayowa is as promiscuous as you appear to think, surely you can see the flaw in me."

Davies frowned slightly. How old was this child again? A child and yet not such a child in most of her viewpoints. Her ability to impassively and succinctly put across the thinly veiled message of how her beauty might be a significant problem here took Davies by surprise. And she had not thought Sade could surprise her anymore. For the umpteenth time, Davies wondered about this student's past life. It was even crazy to think a seventeen-year-old had a past life. She had hardly lived one yet. She was probably the only female in the world who would allude to her looks as an imperfection. She was easily the prettiest girl in the school and one of the most admired. She had also managed to court a few enemies just by the state of being. However, Sade did not appear to care about what anyone thought or felt about her. Chances were, she would attract Mayowa's attention anyway. And that could happen at the Lit evening, interview, or no interview.

"If his reputation is anything to go by," Davies surmised, "he will try it on with whoever interviews him anyway, pretty or not pretty. The important thing is that he doesn't think he can saunter into Queens and do as he pleases. And don't think I don't know what Tito is up to either."

Tito Fernandez, baby sister to Mayowa, was in the same class as Sade and had been her archenemy from day one. Sade had no recollection of having done anything to provoke the dislike. Anne had once told Sade Tito was regarded by all as the prettiest girl in Queens before Sade came four years earlier. Sade had not only stolen that spot but had also made zero attempts to court Tito's friendship. The situation escalated when Tito lost the editorship to Sade in a head-to-head at the beginning of the year. It was their final year in high school. Sade saw Tito and her associates as bullies, another breed she intensely abhorred.

But Tito was the reason Mayowa was coming. He was performing for free at the upcoming Lit evening and allowing them an interview to boot. Tito seemed to think that gave her the right to decide who was good enough to interview her famous big brother. In no uncertain terms, Sade had firmly told Tito it was not up to her, much to the latter's intense annoyance. Tito was big on making someone's dream of meeting Mayowa come true, predictably one of her hangers-on. The implication, of course, was that they could get to date him.

It was all so stupid and irritating. Presumably, if Tito wanted to match make her friend and her brother, she could introduce them. Privately. But no, Tito had to be seen to be a grand puppeteer.

"What Tito wants is of no consequence," Sade said smoothly. "She is not the editor. I am."

Davies nodded happily. Sade was perfect for the job.

"Alright, I will let on you are interviewing to stop all the threats flying around the halls."

"All those threats would only get consolidated and

thrown in one direction. Mine." She made one last attempt to dissuade the principal.

But Davies only gave a small smile.

"Don't be dramatic, Sade. We both know they can only try."

Ever since a thirteen-year-old Sade had walked into her office demanding a placement to continue her education in the prestigious Queens Grammar school, her swollen red eyes telling a story of tears that had dried, Davies had known the girl had no fears. And when she had calmly explained, not threatened, that this was her last point of call before jumping in front of a train at the Oshodi rail track, Davies knew not even death scared her. And that scared Davies more than anything else had ever done before.

Predictably, no sooner was the news out than Tito and friends went up in arms in a war of dirty looks and innuendos. Sade acted oblivious to it all. She was more concerned about Anne, who was disappointed when she heard the news from Sade. Anne had muttered that the interview would have looked great on her CV. Sade was a bit confused. What CV? The girl was going to be a nun.

As the day drew near, between organising the main event, which was the Lit evening, and reviewing articles for the Term magazine, Sade squeezed in some prep for the big interview, getting plenty of help from Anne. Anne had also suggested she tag along for the interview, to, she had quickly added, help with notes, pens, jotters, and a portable recorder. That was fine by Sade. Anne's only other request was that Sade keeps her involvement secret.

"I won't be telling anyone if that's what you mean," Sade had replied. "But I won't be lying about it if anyone directly asks me."

"Like Principal Davies?"

"Yes, like Principal Davies," Sade replied emphatically.

The day had arrived without any further glitch, though. The interview was scheduled for two-thirty that afternoon. As their last class finished at a quarter past two, Sade and Anne hurried to the school hall, whose stage featured a couple of backrooms, one of which was the designated venue for the interview. The hall decorations were almost finished, thanks to the collective efforts of the third and fourth years. The colour theme was lilac and pink.

Carefully navigating through a few streamers and cardboard boxes strewn on the hardwood floor, Sade and Anne made their way towards the fixed stage steps. Sade caught a sudden sinusoidal movement across the floor and stopped stock still in absolute terror. She felt her heart go into overdrive, but her limbs would not obey the higher command to flee. Oblivious to any danger, Anne walked right into an entangled cable, well hidden among cut-out pieces of cardboard and ribbons. With a loud yelp, Anne fell to the floor, arms stretched out in front of her, her school bag partially emptying its contents of the recorder and a few jotters. From the periphery of Sade's vision, she could see a few of the third and fourth years running towards them.

"Are you alright, Anne?" Sade cried out, quickly kneeling beside the smaller girl.

Poor Anne was in tears.

"Sade, my wrist hurts."

Sade looked at the culprit right wrist. It looked

bruised, and there was the beginning of a swelling. Sade helped Anne sit up on the floor. The juniors had gathered around, one of them retrieving items from the floor and putting them back in Anne's bag.

"We need to get you to the school nurse right away."

"What about the interview?" Anne sobbed.

"We'll have to cancel, Anne," Sade said, her gaze so intent on Anne's rapidly swelling wrist that she did not realise there was a sudden quiet in the group of juniors around them until she heard a male voice say behind her:

"There is no need for that. We can do it while the nurse sees to Anne's wrist."

Sade abruptly raised her head to see whom the voice belonged to and stared straight into the eyes of the most beautiful man she ever saw.

Mayowa Fernandez.

Her breath caught in her throat. None of the prep for the interview prepared her for this moment, and not even one of his pictures in the magazines did the same. How did anyone prepare to meet the Mayowa

Fernandez of this world anyway?

Definitely not by half crouching on the floor holding their best friend's swollen wrist!

From where she crouched, Sade could tell he must be over six feet tall, lean, and well-toned. He had deep-set eyes with the inner and outer corners making a straight, horizontally wide line, hooded just the right amount by his brow bone. His brows were thick and nearly formed a monobrow. His nose appeared strong and well defined over moderately full lips. His features were set in a square face. He was caramel-coloured like his sister, a result of their mixed-race heritage. He was wearing a black polo shirt with blue jeans, both snugly fitting on his alluring physique and the contrast against his skin aesthetically pleasing.

"Mayowa Fernandez." Sade let out a deep breath, her voice coming out way more controlled than the clutter she suddenly and unwelcomingly felt inside.

The object of her inner turmoil presently came to half kneel on the other side of Anne.

"Since this is Anne, I assume you are Sade Cole." His voice came out low and husky, his eyes slowly roaming over her face.

Sade could only nod her acknowledgement and turned her face away.

She turned her attention back to Anne and groaned inwardly. Anne looked stunned despite her rapidly swelling wrist, which now frankly looked alarming. Sade did not need to look around at the other Queens Grammar girls to confirm her fears. Principal Davies was right. She turned back to him, her face devoid of any expression.

"I am sorry, but I must get Anne to the sick bay immediately."

"You are right." Mayowa agreed readily, in a pleasant tone. "I will help." He drew his eyes away from her and to Anne's wrist. He grimaced.

"Although I reckon she needs to go to a hospital. She probably needs an x-ray to check that nothing's broken."

"Oh, you don't suppose I have a fracture, do you?" Anne asked, still with the silly dazed look on her face.

Mayowa flashed a dazzling smile, and Sade's heart did a dozen somersaults. He really was ridiculously good-looking!

"Who knows? Come on, let's go get you seen."

Mayowa made an arm sling out of his belt for Anne, insisting she moved her wrist as little as possible. Sade gave him a questioning look, to which he gave a lopsided grin and mouthed *"boys scout"* to her over Anne's head.

They attracted a fair amount of looks and whisperings as they made their way to the sick bay, which was only a hundred metres away, adjacent to the first-year classes.

The matronly-looking nurse glanced at Anne's wrist and declared Anne needed to be taken to the hospital straight away.

"The lit evening," Anne groaned in dismay. "Mrs Tolani, I can't miss it."

"I am sorry, dear," Mrs Tolani said, handing her a couple of painkillers and a glass of water. "But that wrist looks quite nasty, and you are better off seeing a doctor. How did this happen?"

Anne frowned. "I tripped over something and fell on my hands."

"It was a cable wire," Sade added, "moving like a snake." She shuddered.

"A moving cable wire?" Mayowa queried, his brows drawn together. He did not miss Sade's shudder.

In fact, he hardly missed anything about her at all. He had heard a girl's scream from backstage and rushed out to help. He had been stopped in his tracks by the image of the most stunning girl he had ever seen, hunched over a smaller girl, her expression filled with worry and compassion. He could not help staring. When he overheard her suggesting cancelling the interview, realising it was the interview he had been waiting for, he had panicked, which was alien to his nature.

He sussed out she was his interviewer, Sade Cole. He had heard the name several times over dinner at home, usually in derogatory terms from Tito. Tito had never once mentioned the beauty. Not surprising at all. Tito had been irate at losing the editorship to Sade and swore there was something fishy about the girl who turned up out of nowhere to join the prestigious girls-only school in the second year and who, four years on, remained a mystery to everyone. Mayowa silently wondered if there was more to it than that. Was Tito, who all her life had to be in control of everyone and everything around her, intimidated by Sade?

As they made their way over to the sick bay, he had covertly continued his study of her over Anne's head. Mayowa was six foot three, and Sade had to be close to six feet. She was slender, willowy even. She was only a shade darker than he was. Her hair was woven into a single braid that came to rest beyond her slim, graceful neck to the middle of her back. She had an oval face with perfectly shaped eyebrows over dark brown eyes. Full lashes frustratingly hid her expressions from him when he was desperate to know if he had a similar effect on her as she clearly did on him. Her nose was pert in harmony with the oval face and presided over full pink lips. Her cheekbones were elegantly high.

There was an aura about her that did not quite fit into this little girls' school—a maturity beyond her years. Mayowa was nearly twenty but felt like a high school boy.

The arrival of the school minibus to take Anne to the hospital interrupted his thoughts. Mrs Tolani accompanied the patient after delegating the task of manning the sick bay to a younger nurse.

"Right," Sade said, turning to him after the bus had left, Anne's bag slung around her shoulders. "There must be a room about here where we can do this."

The sentence, though uttered in innocence, knocked him for six.

Get your filthy mind out of the gutter, Mayowa Fernandez.

He quickly turned to the new nurse to hide his expressions from Sade. He calmly explained their predicament and asked if there was an examination room, *oh dear lord*, where they could conduct the interview.

The nurse said, of course, gave him an alluring smile, not bothering to disguise her admiration of his male form, and led them to an examination room just down the hall.

They sat comfortably in a reasonably sized, well-lit consulting room a few minutes later. Sade sat in the nurse's chair, and he sat opposite her. His presence was overwhelming, and the room was just too small to contain both of them. *The planet was not big enough...*Sade mused inside.

"Right, let's get this started," she said, putting her recorder on the desk and holding a jotting pad and a pen. She crossed her legs under the desk where he couldn't see them and looked him straight in the eye. Nothing in her demeanour gave away the chaos inside, nor the fact that she tingled all over from scalp to toenails.

He did not flinch from the direct gaze.

"Yes," he agreed smoothly. "Let's get this out of the way."

Chapter Two

The interview lasted a full ninety minutes, but it was not until Sade glanced at her watch as she asked the last question that she realised how fast the time had gone. He was pleasant throughout, assuming no airs, answering her questions easily, and she had found herself relaxing earlier in the conversation. She had started by asking general questions about his earlier years and family before delving into more specific details of his music career from a very young age. He was a lyric tenor like Justin Timberlake.

She was pleasantly surprised to learn he played several instruments, spoke three languages, and was a member of Mensa. He was in his second year at the University studying Music. He admitted with a self-mocking smile that he was hopeless at basketball, a sport he loved, and average at best in football and athletics. If his music career ever went downhill, he would not be looking into sports.

Well, you can't have it all... Sade thought with a

touch of envy. People like him had it all handed to them on a platter of gold, the right genes, into the right family. How could they not look down at ordinary folks who had nothing?

"Thank you for taking time out of your busy schedule for this interview," she said sincerely. "And indeed, for your contributions to our Lit day this year."

"No worries, I will gladly do it again." He smiled. "I am quite famished. Do you fancy a grab to eat?"

The unexpected question surprised Sade. She couldn't….didn't want to fraternise with him. Aside from the fact that he was brother to the despicable Tito, not that that was his fault, he was still Mayowa Fernandez.

Carefully arranging her equipment into Anne's little bag, she politely declined the offer.

"Why not?" he asked softly. Suddenly the atmosphere in the room changed. Whatever it was that had been simmering beneath the surface was now threatening out. Sade was not exactly sure what it was, but it had to be caged. And then shot in the head.

She slowly looked up at him. "I barely have time

as it is to prepare for the Lit evening."

He nodded thoughtfully. "What about tonight? Will you be my date? Pretty please?"

She stared at him and said the first thing that came to her head. "You can't have a date. You are the performing artiste."

He chuckled. "Thanks for stating the obvious. After my performance, can we go somewhere quiet and talk?"

Sade took a deep breath to take over control of the whole ridiculous conversation. *Talk about what*

She stood up and stepped around the desk.

"No," she replied.

"Again, why not?"

"What makes you think I don't already have plans for the evening?"

He frowned. "Cancel them. Be with me."

Ha! She knew it. He had a wart somewhere. His arrogance rankled. From the look on his face, she realised he was genuinely surprised she did not want any further association with him. Not that she had any specific plans for the evening, but that was not even the point, was it?

"And why should I do such a silly thing?" She said in sheer disbelief.

"Hanging out with me is not a silly thing."

That was debatable, she thought but said instead. "Cancelling my initial plans just to be with you is. Besides, I do not even want to hang out with you. I am not one of your fans. Bye."

She turned her back to him and walked towards the door. There was no use in continuing this pointless argument.

He moved pretty fast for someone who claimed to be an average athlete. Sade was closer to the door than he was, but he got to it first. And effectively blocked her exit, his lean, tall frame casually leaning against the door.

She stared at him. "Mayowa, I…open the door…."

"Never mind that. Please just explain that part about not being a fan."

"Simple, I do not like your style."

"What would it take to get you?"

She blinked. "I beg your pardon?"

"What would it take to have you as a fan?"

His proximity was making it difficult to think clearly. She could smell him, breathe him, and he was turning her brain into mush. She shook her head.

"It doesn't matter. You are you."

"Nevertheless, you have an opinion. I am just interested in your thoughts."

"I, for one, think you should have a stage name!" Sade blurted out. "For some mystery."

"Stage name like?" Mayowa asked.

"Be a Lynx, private and mysterious."

"The cat or the mythology?"

"Both." She replied.

He smiled. "I like it, the name that is. Any more ideas?"

"Yes," she looked pointedly at the door behind him. "You'd open the door so that I can leave."

"Which brings us back to our date."

"We do not have a date." She stressed each word for effect.

He shrugged a tad dismissively. "Look, I am an honest bloke. I like you. I liked you from the second I saw you."

Sade was not impressed. He met her only a couple of hours ago. She expected he said that to all the girls. Mayowa had something of a Don Juan reputation, and Sade was a firm believer in there being no smokes without fire.

"Thank you," she said icily and pointedly looked at her watch. "I need to get going."

"Sure." He said calmly. He somewhat sensed he had overstepped a boundary. "Can I just say hello later in the evening then?"

"Maybe." She said unconvincingly. She had no intention of meeting him later or at any other time in this lifetime.

"That's good enough for me," Mayowa said, shifting his frame from the door so she could leave. He was sure she had no plans to see him again. One way or the other, he had to convince her he was worth getting to know.

*****

The literary evening, Lit, for short, was the most

prestigious annual social event at Queens Grammar school. Historically the press club and the Literary society were interwoven, and the student officers were mostly the same. While membership was open to all, holding office was only attained through a highly selective and rigorous process.

Sade had had to leave Anne, who had returned from the hospital with a plaster cast on her wrist, behind in the dormitory. She had no plans to stay longer than was necessary in her role as the editor and told Anne so.

She wore a knee-length red double-breasted blazer dress that was a birthday gift from Anne the year before. Her hair was tightly packed behind her ears in a bun. She wore a pair of hoop earrings. She did not own a chain and always left her neck bare. She also owned little make-up and judiciously stretched it out for as long as possible. She wore low-heel black sandals and held a small brown office file containing her welcome speech.

The third and fourth years had outdone themselves, and Sade could barely recognise the hall she had left only a few hours before. The stage backdrop was a magnificent golden drape with the school logo of Queen Moremi in the centre, brought nearly to life with great floodlight. The stage was about three feet high, flanked by a small stairway on either side. The great walls had existing artworks from several generations of massively talented fine art students.

There were decorated round tables and chairs on the floor in lilac and pink with matching centrepieces, table covers, and serviette papers, and a central clearing in the big hall for the girls and their invited friends to dance later.

She made a mental note to commend the third and fourth years in the following school publication.

The evening was a huge success. The girls milled around in elegant evening dresses. They were mostly from elitist families who shopped for designer wear abroad. Their dates were from similar high-end schools. No one wanted to hang out with a loser. Sade had never allowed anyone close enough to find out anything about her. Not even Anne. A lone Sade was not an unusual sight, but a solitary Patricia was.

Patricia was one of Tito's allies, and rumours going around was that she had a schoolgirl crush on Mayowa, and Tito had allegedly blessed the union, which made for a big laugh indeed.

A guy like Mayowa had no problems picking girls, and the world was filled with beautiful women. Sade Cole had no intention of being a number in his tally.

The object of her thoughts was singing one of his current hits. Mayowa became a pop star at fifteen. He was also a songwriter and wrote most of his songs. His live performances were few, and this was the first time he was singing at a high school event, and everyone knew Tito was to be thanked for that.

He was gifted; Sade had to give it to him. His voice was true and did not need any enhancement. His performance was flawless and captivating, and Sade knew to admit to herself when she was wrong. She had become a fan. But an apocalyptic event would have to be on the cards before she would admit that to him. Not that the opportunity would ever arise anyway.

Having done her speech, Sade decided to listen to one more song and head back to the dormitory. She knew Anne was absolutely gutted about missing out and would be glad to see her. Misery loving company and all.

As the next song ended, Sade finished her soda and made her way through the little crowd towards the doorway. She was nearly at the exit door when she heard her name. She swirled around on autopilot and almost bumped into him. He really was quick on his feet.

"You are leaving." It sounded like an accusation.

She said nothing. She was conscious of the stares around them and a quiet. The dangerous type. She even felt the elusive grapevine, looking and listening in.

"Sade, please don't leave yet," he looked around him a bit frantically and scratched his head as if looking for the right words to change her mind. Sade knew they did not exist.

"I have to get back to Anne," Sade told him.

"She will be fine," Mayowa said quickly. "Just don't go. Don't leave me."

She was not leaving him. He was not hers to leave. She was simply leaving a party.

"Sorry," she said, feeling anything but sorry, as she turned her back to him. Against her will, her vision became blurred from a film of tears. He was too much, too much like *him*. She would not allow him to get to her. She would never be like her mother.

Chapter Three

Sade turned over to the next page of her biology textbook. Up till a few minutes ago, she had actually been enjoying reading the murky details of the human digestive system.

She was lying prone on the upper bunk bed. The lower bunk belonged to Anne. Anne had gone out to lunch with her parents.

Sade was doing her best to ignore the girl standing close by.

"Sade, did you even hear what I just said?"

"I do not have to dignify you with a response." She replied through tight lips.

"This is not about me. My brother…"

"Is a crazy man."

Tito scowled. "I happen to think so too. Especially after the way you publicly humiliated him." Her voice dripped with venom. "Look, I am no more thrilled about this than you are. He can't very well walk into a girls' dorm by himself, and I am only doing this because I owe him one. That one being for coming to perform at your Lit evening!"

"Good thing then that I do not owe you anything. Go look for someone else to even scores with your brother."

"Whatever." Tito shrugged. "Stay and hide here like a coward for all of eternity."

Sade spun around on the bed to glare at the other girl's retreating back. She did not hide from anyone. She reached for a red jumper and pulled it over her camisole.

"Look Mayowa, I am sorry. But she wouldn't even move an inch."

Tito was, however, surprised to see a wide grin spreading across her brother's face instead. Both siblings were standing just outside of Sade's dormitory.

"I think you have been quite successful, Tito. Look behind you."

Tito looked over her shoulder and saw Sade striding towards them.

She turned back to her brother. "Now we are even. Don't try to make me do anything this stupid again. I have got a reputation to protect. What if my friends had seen me helping you out with Miss-Goody-Two-Shoes?"

"You will live," Mayowa assured her. "Now, do run along to the parents."

It was three Saturdays after the lit evening and Queen's school visiting day. It was a lovely sunny afternoon. He had thought little else apart from Sade the last three weeks. Her face hounded him the way nothing ever had before. She was his first thought in the morning and the last before he dropped off to sleep at night. He had written more songs than he had in the previous year.

He watched her stride towards him in a red sweater over a pair of blue jeans. She did not look too pleased. His heart pounded away. He swallowed hard.

She came to stand in front of him, her arms neatly folded across her chest.

"Hi," she said in a silky voice.

"Hi, you too. How have you been?"

"I didn't think I would see you again."

He grinned. "I am not easy to get rid of. Ask Tito."

"Your sister and I don't roll. What do you want, Mayowa?"

"You. I want you. I like you."

His gaze was fully on her face, roving over her brows to the long thick lashes, her high cheekbones, to her beautiful mouth. He longed to kiss her pink lips. He knew he was dying to hold her in his arms. He did not understand how anyone could make another feel this way and not feel anything themselves. He kept his hands firmly in his trouser pockets for control but did not attempt to hide the dark desire in his eyes. Deliberately.

"I am not in the dating market. Try my next life?" Sade said flippantly.

"I thought you might say something like that," he smiled, refusing to betray the hurt he felt at her words. "So, I thought I'd ask you to be my friend. You know, just friends."

"There is no such animal as just friends between someone like you and someone like me."

He was momentarily taken aback. What kind of a person did she think he was?

"There can be." His gaze did not waver. "Just get to know me, the real me, not whatever it is you might have heard or read."

"And?" she asked suspiciously.

"And if there is more between us, it wouldn't all be my doing."

Sade inched closer. "What are you trying to say?"

"It's easy for you to refuse to date me from a distance. It won't be so easy saying no after getting to know me."

Sade was genuinely astounded.

"Are you always this sure of your appeal?"

"The truth is," he made a fist inside his pockets to keep his hands from reaching out to pull her to him and kissing the senses out of her head just so she was sure of his appeal. "I've never really given too much thought to it. I assume it is there. Don't we all have something appealing about us?"

"Go on."

"Just hang out with me a couple of times. If you still don't even want to be friends, then I will leave you alone."

"Forever?"

"Sure." Mayowa lied through his teeth. He would find ways to convince her he was perfect for her.

"Okay." Sade looked away to hide her amusement, convinced she had found a way to get rid of him. And it was all his own idea.

*****

"I have never had a haircut."

"Never?"

"Hmm," Sade nodded, digging her teeth into a chicken leg. She was surprised that the vegetarian Tito had a carnivore brother. Apart from being obviously good-looking, the two siblings could not be more different.

After their little wager, Mayowa had told Sade he had brought along a picnic basket. They were sitting on a lovely blue geometric patterned blanket on the football field, devouring a feast of stir fry rice, well-seasoned and quite tasty barbecued chicken, steak meat, mixed fruit salad and fresh juice.

Now and then, she watched him from underneath

her eyelashes. He was wearing a navy-blue short sleeve tight-fitting top with black denim jeans. It was always going to be impossible to ignore that he was drop-dead gorgeous. It was a good thing almost all the girls had gone off with their families for the afternoon.

"That was a delicious meal. Thanks."

"Pleasure's all mine," Mayowa said, tidying up after them. Sade helped him put the plates and cutleries back in the basket.

He lay on his back, staring at the skies.

"I am pretty sure it is not alright to lie back after such a big meal," Sade teased him.

He gave her a lopsided grin. "See, you are already caring about my welfare."

She laughed. It was nice to have someone on this visiting day. Not that she really had him, of course, but the illusion was nice on this day.

He came to lie on his side facing her. "You said you didn't like my music the other day."

"Did I? Were those really my words?"

"You said you weren't a fan. Same thing."

Sade stared into the distance, choosing her words

carefully, aware she had his full attention.

"I think your voice is incredible, and your range is insane. You must know you are immensely talented."

"Sade, are you complimenting me?" he asked incredulously.

She shook her head. "No, these are facts."

The light dawned in his eyes. "It's the music I produce you are not a fan of."

Sade shrugged. "Your music is nice, I suppose."

"But…"

She turned back to look at him. "It's the Americanisation for me. Like you must sing like Americans to sell records. Where is the originality, though?"

He sat upright. "You do know I am half American, right?"

Sade did not baulk. "You do realise there are like literally thousands of American artistes you have to compete with on the world stage? How are you going to beat them at their own game? They grew up in that music culture. You didn't. However," she raised her right index finger. "You do have an edge."

"Which is?"

"The languages here are quite tonal. Yoruba is one. And there are other music genres around you which will be complementary to your voice. You can bring something fresh to the rest of the world. Listen."

She closed her eyes and hummed one of her father's songs for a few minutes whilst he listened intently, bolt upright.

"You have a lovely voice, Sade. Oh my God, that is incredible!"

She ignored that and instead taught him the lyrics to the song. He sang it out loud. His voice carried on the wind and twirled the grasses. The birds stopped chirping and listened to him. Sade was mesmerised.

"It's Afrobeat, Sade. I love Afrobeat. Fela is my idol! I have not heard this song before. Whose is it?"

Sade lowered her lashes quickly, so he missed the pain. "I don't know," she lied. "But it sounds cool, right?"

"Cool? It's terrific, and you can sing, Sade. I mean, I suspected it but hearing it…." He made a show of dying on the fields, and she laughed again, a deep throaty laugh that tugged sharply on his heart.

"You are killing this prince," he said in a whisper.

She ignored him again and looked up at the skies. "The sun's setting. I better get back to my dormitory."

"I will walk you."

She shook her head. "The other girls will be coming back soon. I don't want them to...."

"See you with me?" He grimaced. "That bad?"

"There is a grapevine...." She started, seeking for the first time to soothe his ego.

"Say no more. I have indeed heard the legend of this grapevine. Tito swore it's you."

Sade smiled. "I am beginning to think it's a myth, to be honest. If there's one, I would know."

"As the journalist?"

She nodded.

"Is that what you want to be? A journalist? Print media?"

He sounded somewhat disappointed.

"Hey, journalism is a cool career." She defended vehemently.

"Of course, it is. It's you. I think you should be on

TV. You are intelligent, beautiful, and an amazing interviewer; your voice is terrific. I see a TV show with your name written all over it."

"Maybe," Sade said noncommittally as she rolled up the blanket and handed it to him to put back in the basket. He reached for her hand.

"Sade, please, when can I see you again?"

She squinted from the glare of the late afternoon sun.

"I am busy. Exams."

"I know. I will wait till after exams."

*****

He was there on the last day of the term. Waiting just outside of her dormitory.

"I am here to take you home."

Sade looked anxiously about her. The other girls were wheeling luggage out and casting several glances their way. Sade was too distressed to dwell on that, and Mayowa did not seem to notice them.

Chauffeurs were running towards the girls to relieve them of their baggage. They had come to take their bosses' daughters home.

Home.

Where was home?

"Tito said no one comes to visit you, and no one comes to take you home. You always go back by yourself."

Sade turned her back to him, stiffening up.

"Tito should learn to mind her business."

"Also, I'd like to see you during the holidays. It helps if I know where you live. My car is parked just outside the gates. Please let me take you home."

"I am perfectly capable of getting home, all by myself, thank you. And I don't recall inviting you to my home."

She walked away from him back to her dormitory, knowing he could not follow her. At some point, he was bound to leave, and go back to where he came from. At some point, he was bound to leave her alone. Her bags were all packed too. But just to exit the dormitory.

Mayowa watched her stomp off in bewilderment. He could have sworn she was starting to like him a little, and they were making some progress in their friendship. He, of course, had no intention to allow her friendzone him, given how he felt about her.

He was not sure what he would say to her when she was ready to go home, but he had to undo whatever damage had just been done, and he needed to make plans to see her in the next six weeks. The afternoon turned to the early evening, and as it got dark, he started to worry. What was she still doing in there? It was all very bizarre.

He paced back and forth outside the dorm, wondering whether to shout out her name and ask if she was alright. She had to be the only girl left in the dorm. It was not safe. It did not occur to him that he may be the reason she did not feel safe.

Sade watched him through the little gaps in the windows. Eventually, he would leave. For home. For America. For wherever people went and never came back.

But he was not budging. Stubborn as a mule. Equally determined, Sade told herself she would have to be more brutal. He would eventually get the message. It was getting dark, and she had to leave. She picked up her two bags and walked out, determined to pretend he was not there. He immediately fell in step with her.

"Let me help with the bags, Sade."

Expectedly, she ignored him and marched on. To her own version of home, which was a one-bedroom apartment in the principal's boys' quarters. She was allowed to stay here only during the holidays.

She stopped in front of the apartment to get the keys out of her pocket. She didn't have to look at him to see a million questions on his face. They became daggers in his eyes, flying out at her, and she could feel them piercing her skin like a physical thing.

She put the key in the lock to open the door and then turned to acknowledge him. He was standing just under the light hanging over the door.

"Mayowa, you must leave now. You can't come in here with me."

"Like hell, I can't! What is this place?" He waved his arms about. "What are we doing here?"

"An excellent question indeed," she answered in

her most dismissive tone, "if you'd just substitute we for I."

She pushed open the door with her right foot, walked into the apartment, dropped the bags on the floor, flicked on the light switch, and tried to close the door to his face. From experience, she was not at all surprised when his lithe form was already on the undesired side of the door.

"Ah no, Sade," he shook his head. "You will not close that door on me. Let us get something straight," he looked around the small room. There was a study desk and chair beside a double bed, above which was a wall-mounted clothes rack. A transistor radio graced the desktop. "There is no way I am leaving you here all alone."

He turned to her; puzzlement written all over his sinfully handsome face. "How come no one comes for you anyway? Are your folks that mean?"

Sade felt his words as a physical punch to a region just below her heart. All that she had bottled up for years rose unbidden into her throat and gathered as tears, making their way down her cheeks. The willpower that held back the pain and anguish abandoned her when she needed it most.

"Oh my God, Sade." Mayowa swiftly pulled her into his arms. "I am sorry. I am sorry I said that. It is obvious I am an idiot. I didn't mean to hurt you. I am sorry."

Her head came to settle on his chest as she sobbed uncontrollably. Deep inside, she found her wounds were still raw. She held on to him till the tears ebbed, aware that his shirt collar was soaked with her tears. She felt devoid of energy, and her legs were weak, barely supporting the upright position. She drew away from him and sat on the bed. He pulled the chair and sat opposite her, holding both of her hands in his.

"You can tell me all about it," he began, and as she started to shake her head, added, "whenever you are ready to. I will be listening."

She pulled her hands away. It had been very comfortable, too comfortable in his arms.

"Thank you," she looked at him. "For the offer. But I'd like to be alone now."

"Sade, please don't." He said almost helplessly.

"Don't ask me to leave you alone in this state. Don't push me away. I am begging you not to ask this of me."

For the first time, she saw his vulnerability. She saw what he felt for her in his eyes, and the intensity of it was like nothing she had ever seen before. And even more worrisome was that she…she liked it. She liked him.

"What kind of a person are you?"

"The kind who is madly in love with you."

She was speechless. Her heart skipped a beat before going into overdrive. He held her gaze steadily.

"From the moment that I saw you, I fell for you. And I love it. I love the way you make me feel. I love you."

He leaned over, incapable of any further control, and his mouth took over hers. Sade reeled from the impact. He was the best thing she had ever tasted, and she tingled all over from a billion sensations. She kissed him back with a fervour that astonished her, pulling him closer to her until they both tumbled onto the bed. Her arms went out of their own volition around his neck, and her fingers buried themselves in his afro-style hair. He groaned as her tongue twirled around his, and he wrapped his arms around her waist to pull her up even closer to his toned body. One hand cupped her behind, and the other journeyed up through her top to unhook her bra. Her breath got caught in her throat when she felt his fingers on her left breast and nipple, and then a few minutes later, both hands cupped both breasts. He neatly disposed of her top baring her chest to him.

She was breathtakingly beautiful. Mayowa dipped his mouth to a nipple, and she moaned out loudly. She was powerless to control her own body, this burning desire that threatened to consume her whole. Swiftly disposing of all items of their clothing, he covered every inch of her body with his touch, his body and his love.

It was sweet torture, the pain of becoming a woman, his loving and even hearing him say how much he loved her, knowing how vastly different his world was to hers.

Moments later, when sanity and reality kicked in, Sade could not believe what they had done. He nuzzled her neck gently.

"Did I hurt you, my love?"

She shook her head.

"Please tell me it was beautiful for you too."

"It was." Was that her voice?

"I will make you happy, Sade. I swear, I will always make you happy."

She smiled at him, her face not betraying the general distrust she held inside.

"I stay here during the holidays. This is my home."

He swallowed hard. *This* was not normal.

"What about food?"

"Principal Davies," Sade replied shortly.

"And…"

"Please, Mayowa, could you not ask too many questions? And please do not say anything to your sister about this place." Sade implored.

He let out a breath he had not been aware of holding in. He had his arm around her waist and slowly massaged her navel.

"I won't," he promised. "I know what Tito is like. But she also knows what I am like. She will not bother you anymore."

He kissed the top of her head and added, "whenever you want to talk about it, I will be listening. But we can hang out here during your holidays. I have an apartment close to the university, and you can come and visit me there as well, anytime."

She chuckled slightly, an image of the bad-boy pop star staying in this dingy with a teenage schoolgirl popping into her head.

"Is it funny? That I want to be with you so bad."

She shook her head. "You are a pop star."

"Not with you, though. I am not that. I am a boy in love with this girl who just can't seem to take him seriously."

He tickled her belly, and she wriggled and laughed out aloud.

She acknowledged that she was happy at that moment. The happiest in her life, and that was enough. It was unexpected, given her life up to that moment. This was her best moment. Things could only get worse.

Later, they went out for a takeaway dinner which

they devoured in his car. Back in her room, he talked about things they should do and places they could visit during the holidays.

"We should definitely go on a boat to Tarkwa bay beach. You will love it." He said.

He had no idea multiple alarm bells were ringing in her head. He was Mayowa Fernandez, a celebrity. She was Sade Cole, a homeless nobody.

Men like Mayowa, *like him*, do not belong to one woman for all time. She would never be the property of a man. She would never owe her life to anyone.

As he made plans, he sounded so happy she did not have the heart to tell him she could not be a part of his world, nor did she have the energy to argue the why not. She could not self-destroy. Her life would not be taken out of her hands and would not hinge on the whims of a man. No matter how rich or ridiculously good-looking he was…especially if he was rich and ridiculously good-looking.

*****

Mayowa woke up several hours later with a smile

on his face. They had made love two more times during the night, and they were even more glorious than their first time. He had never felt this happy in his entire life. The deed had been done, boundaries dismantled, and surely Sade was now his woman. He had won the girl over finally.

She obviously had hidden layers and depths, but he was confident they would all come unpeeled with time. He reached out for her and felt emptiness next to him. He sat bolt upright, suddenly fully awake. He was alone in the room. She was gone, and so were her bags and the transistor radio.

He hurriedly put on his clothes and searched all over the school grounds, but she was truly gone.

She strolled out of his life just as she had strolled in to interview him.

It was as though she had never really been there.

Chapter Four

Nine years later

“Amazing as usual, Sade,” Tony, her producer, called with a thumbs up as they wrapped up the tenth episode of the Cole show.

“Thanks, Tony.”

Her guest was the president of the academic staff union of universities, Dr Tega Okosun. The union was on strike again, and the university students were home. Most of the issues, though alarming, were not new, and as such, the crucial concern by the different tiers of government to work towards lasting solutions was non-existent. A generation of the future workforce was barely getting a decent education, while the offspring of politicians and the elite were getting world-class education in ivy league schools abroad. It was a truly shameful situation.

Sade touched on the key points, and Tega expanded on them, proposing solutions and tests of change, some of which she zoomed in on, asking him for further clarifications.

The production also included a pre-recorded filming of a few university students working at odd jobs during the strike, one of whom was peddling on the streets of Lagos. Sade asked rhetorically if this would be the future of the poor working-class kids.

Sade thanked Tega for coming as she walked him off the set, between the camera equipment and the crew.

As she waved him off, Tony came to stand by her side.

"Come on, kid. We should celebrate!"

Sade considered this. "Celebrate what?"

"The tenth show, of course! You are a hit. Everyone loves you. The camera loves you; the crew, your guests, and management, oh management." Tony crossed his arms on his chest. "They love the ratings. Whatever were you doing in print?"

"Don't dismiss the power of the pen, Tony." Sade waved a finger at him. She had loved her time in print media. But the readership had dwindled and narrowed to a demography that was also diminishing, given the life expectancy. The young gravitated towards television and the internet. The paper she had been working with until three months prior had closed, and she was lucky to get this new job at ACE network. Granted, ACE headhunted her from her previous powerful write-ups and offered her the job on strong references from her previous bosses. Still, she felt fortunate to have this. Her transition to television had gone more smoothly than she had thought it would. After the first show, Tony commented that she was born to be in front of the cameras.

And someone else had thought so too in a previous life; the thought came unbidden. She forcefully pushed it into the back of her mind. This was her life now.

"Some of us are going out tonight, maybe hit a nightclub? You should come with us." Tony interrupted her musings.

Sade shook her head automatically, looking at her watch pointedly.

"Time to go home, Tony."

"Sure." Tony backed off. Sade was predictable in

this respect. "If you change your mind, you have my number."

"Have fun!" Sade replied, turning her back to him and heading towards make-up. She always took off her make-up before leaving for home.

Home.

Now she had one.

With people.

A real one.

And she loved her home.

She loved her life now.

The Lagos traffic, as usual, was unbecoming, and she arrived home quite late.

Teju was watching TV in the living room. It was a large spacious room with modern décor of mainly neutrals. The sofa was a long beige C-shaped corner sofa, recliner at either end, with brown flower-patterned scattered cushions. The flooring was a rustic oak with a centre plush, rich chocolate rug on top of which was a coffee table. A big TV hung on the wall across the sofa, with a full-motion mount. The curtains were dark sand blackout eyelets spanning French doors and windows. There were a couple of pictures on the wall, one of Femi, on the first day of school that term. There was one of Sade and Femi on a boat cruise on the river Seine a day after Femi's seventh birthday. There was another of the two of them with Teju at Sade's university graduation. Femi was five at the time. Large decorative floor flowers in planters graced either side of the sofa. There was an adjoining dining room before the kitchen.

"Hi, auntie," Sade plopped onto the sofa, stretching her slender form along its long axis.

"How are you, Sade? You look quite tired." The older woman looked at her, a frown creasing her forehead.

"It's the traffic, auntie. I am fine."

"Well, your dinner is in the microwave."

"Thank you. I will check in on Femi first and then have a warm shower."

Teju nodded. "Good idea. Make sure he is still breathing."

Sade laughed at the hint of her over-protectiveness.

Teju came into her life nine years earlier, at an

opportune time. And had taken over the role of the mother Sade lost years before. Teju had taken nearly all the physical burden off her young shoulders and tried to relieve the emotional ones as much as possible. She swore she needed Sade more than Sade needed her. Sade remained unconvinced of that nonsense, of course. Teju saved her.

Sade called her auntie, but they had no blood relationship. What they had was stronger. Teju was in her late fifties, had a full figure and was ebony coloured. She was several inches shorter than Sade and looked a decade younger than her age. She attracted a decent male interest and had a more fascinating social life than Sade, a point they argued about constantly. Teju did not understand how anyone could be a TV personality and yet live the life of a recluse. And how would she ever find love if she didn't give any man a chance?

Teju had been married before and was not interested in going down that path again. But Sade had not been and was not even trying.

"Not all men are bad."

"Maybe." Sade had replied vaguely in the familiar tone which signified that was as much as she had to say on the subject. Teju knew the Cole wall when she saw it.

Sade sighed contently as the warm water poured down her skin. Femi was sleeping soundly and breathing just fine.

They were all happy now, and that was all anyone really needed.

*****

Monday morning had Sade preparing materials for her eleventh show – on the ills of internet scammers called yahoo–yahoo boys, the devaluation of the traditional moral system and the celebration of ill-gotten wealth.

Her office was at the end of a long corridor on the first floor of the ACE building. She had chosen it primarily for its distance from the hustle and bustle of the TV network. It was not an office anyone came to on a detour. You had to have a purpose for seeking her out. It was a medium-sized office with windows overlooking the car park, and so was a short walk to and from parking, which meant she did not have to socialise unnecessarily before and after work.

Three walls were painted teal, but the accent wall behind her desk was salmon. She had a big dark rectangular desk directly facing the door on which sat a laptop computer and stationery holder. To her right was a small bookshelf. There was a home-sized printer under her desk for small job printing. She also had a swivel chair as she liked a little spinning when she contemplated her ideas.

As the day went by, her desk tended to get messier, but she always tidied up before leaving so she could return to a welcoming office the next day.

So it was that her desk was still tidy on Monday morning when her mobile rang. It was Tony.

"Hi, Tony. All okay?" She asked.

"Good morning, Sade. Can you join me in Kenny's office in fifteen?" Tony sounded quite formal.

Kenny Lawal was the executive producer and had his hands on quite a few projects. He generally trusted the Cole show to Tony and was pleased with the take-off of the show and the ratings.

"Sure, Tony."

She had only ever been to Kenny's office twice before. One was before her first show, and the second was after it. Tony had assured her that although Kenny generally appeared to be hands off the show, he was up to date with all they did.

Kenny's office was centrally located and right in the hub of all the network's activities. It was a big room with through and through masculine décor. Kenny was a big man, literally speaking, and he took over any room he was in.

He waved them to sit opposite him after exchanging the standard pleasantries.

He was not a man that bushed around the bush.

"You might both be aware Primetime entertainment is hosting an afrobeats music festival next month."

Tony nodded. Sade said nothing.

Primetime acquired the ACE network a few months before she joined ACE and pumped quite a lot of money into ACE, which allowed them to expand, improve production and employ more staff. And to headhunt for talents like her and pay attractive high wages.

Everyone knew about the music festival, of course. Some of her crew, including Tony, had acquired tickets weeks ago. Top afrobeats artistes across the continent were signed up to perform. It was expected to be the biggest music festival on the continent. It was also the first of its kind, and talk was that it was set to be an annual event.

"They have also successfully added another A-lister to perform." Kenny paused for effect. Sade was unsure what for but was willing to wait for it.

"Who?" Tony could hardly contain his excitement.

It certainly did not occur to him to wonder what it had to do with them, Sade ruminated.

"Lynx," Kenny said with a wide grin.

Sade felt the blood draining from her face and a big lump rising into her throat. Even the seat she sat on seemed to twirl a bit.

Oblivious to her distress, Tony did a little dance in his seat.

Kenny went on. "But that's not why you are both here," he turned to Sade and noticed she looked a little pale.

"Sade, are you okay?"

She nodded curtly, unable to speak.

"He's granting his first TV interview, and Primetime has asked that it be on the Cole show. Guys, this is huge given Sade's very short TV career."

Sade felt physically sick. She was going to be sick. Even Tony was shocked.

"Lynx does not do interviews." He said to Kenny.

Kenny spread out his hands. "I don't know what Primetime has got on him, but I am not one to look a gift horse in the mouth, guys. This is the biggest artiste to come out of Africa. Sade, are you sure you are okay?"

No, she was not.

She shook her head and finally found her voice. "It does not make sense. My show, why my show? My show ponders hard-core social issues. Musical artistes? Not my genre."

Both Tony and Kenny stared at her in utter

disbelief.

"We are talking about Lynx, Sade," Tony said slowly. "L-Y-N-X."

Sade rolled her eyes. She invented the damn name!

Kenny considered her for a moment. "Your show is new and is malleable. I get what you are saying. We can spin this. What about homeboy made good on the world stage? A role model for young people to pass on that vital message that they can become successful with raw talent and not need to internet scam anyone. I like that idea, by the way. Too many crooks out there. The important thing is we can spin this to align with your ideals, right?"

Wrong, Sade thought in panic. This was all wrong. She had an intense sense of Déjà vu. How was this even happening again?

Kenny continued. "You are the hottest, freshest look on TV. Gosh, the aesthetics of you and Lynx on set alone! Primetime knows this. They specifically asked for you. And like I said, we can spin this."

Tony put his hands together. "You are doing great, Sade. I am grateful for the day you walked into ACE.

Don't be nervous. We can do this. We will do the prep together."

Sade looked at the two men. She saw their perspective. It was also about their career, after all. Lynx's music was recognised across the globe, and getting an international A-lister on to shows on ACE was incredible. And a first TV interview from a celebrity who had refused to give one for years could not be turned down.

They could not see her perspective. No one could. Something said on a football field years ago, added with granting a first TV interview now, three months into her television career, was all too much of a coincidence.

And everyone knew there was no such animal.

The question was, why?

"I have not got a choice, have I?"

Kenny shook his head. "Not really. You are…" he said slowly, "an interesting person, Sade. I don't know anyone else who would not grab this opportunity by the balls. I can pass on your point of view to management, but I doubt it will make any difference."

Sade knew when to retreat and re-strategise. She and the man dubbed America's sexiest had only met on three occasions. Oh, but that third time, Sade groaned inwardly.

There had been loads of women after her. Their night together must be a faint memory for him, if that.

"Sure, let's do Lynx," she said.

*****

Sade massaged the back of her neck with her left hand. She had never felt tenser in her life. As doomsday drew nearer, she felt more and more unwell inside with unease. Nothing felt right. Tony had never seen her like this during prep for a show, and he was starting to get worried. She sometimes appeared distracted and, at other times, short-tempered. He had expressed some concerns to Kenny, who assured him that even Sade was human and was bound to be a bit nervous about interviewing the Lynxes of this world.

Tony had come up with the idea that they worked on the final prep in his office, which, thank God, was not the last stop before the end of the world that her office was.

They were both working, seated next to each other on a couch, a coffee table in front of them, on which Tony's laptop was placed. It was three days before the interview.

He had felt the couch would be more relaxing to work at than his desk. He was wrong. He watched as she massaged her neck. He could see how tense her muscles were. He sighed and minimised the page. Immediately the screen came alive with Lynx's attractive features.

Sade startled. "Since when did he become your wallpaper?"

"Since he became my priority one," Tony replied with a disarming smile. "Come here."

He turned her back to him and started massaging her neck and shoulder muscles. He was pretty good and was rewarded as she began to relax. They were both oblivious to a little commotion that had just started outside on the corridors.

"Oh, you are quite good," Sade murmured.

He chuckled. "My mum had back pains when I was

younger. We boys took turns to massage her back."

"I take it you don't have a sister?" She asked.

"No, we…" A loud knock on the door interrupted his response.

"Come in," he called out without taking his eyes off his current masseur mission.

The door opened to admit Kenny into the room. They both looked up at him in surprise, Tony's hands still on her shoulders. Sade knew that Kenny and Tony met regularly to discuss the show. They were, however, not expecting him this morning. He took only a step in, his large frame in the doorway.

"Come in," Sade said, noticing how tense he was.

But before Kenny could take another step, the atmosphere behind him seemed to take on a life all of its own, and in a split second, he was there.

Lynx.

Time stood stock-still for a few seconds, and then like a whirlwind, nine years flew out through the window behind her, the power of it rocking her like a hurricane did a ship.

"Hi, Sade," he said in his most unfriendly tone.

Chapter Five

She could only gape at him in horrified disbelief. The summation of all her worst nightmares had come to life.

He moved past Kenny to insinuate himself in the room. His eyes settled on Tony's hands on her shoulders for a few seconds, then back to her face.

"Excuse us," he said tersely without even looking at him.

Spluttering something incoherent, Tony jumped off the couch and, in the process, sent some papers flying across the room. He bent down to quickly retrieve them, muttering something about Mary, Joseph, and Jesus, before making a fast exit after the retreating Kenny.

Sade closed her eyes, counted to ten, and opened them.

"I am still here." He drawled with a hint of an American accent. He drew a chair from under Tony's desk and came to sit across from her, with only the coffee table between them. He looked like he had just stepped out of GQ magazine in a navy-blue pinstripe three-piece suit.

He stared at her uncomfortably; one could almost say rudely. His expression was unfathomable.

"You are even more beautiful than I remember." He said finally.

That knocked her for six. It did not somehow feel like a compliment.

"You remember?" She asked and felt foolish, even as the words fell out of her mouth.

"Trust me; you are not forgettable. Not after that Houdini stunt you pulled, especially not after I was the last one seen with you."

Sade flinched.

"I made a phone call…." She began, but he cut her off.

"Not to me. Nevertheless, it exonerated me from charges of kidnap, possibly murder."

"That bad?" she heard her voice come out in a croak.

He nodded. But even that was not as bad as the pain of a broken heart.

She did not know what to say. Her heart was beating so loudly she was afraid he would hear. She had to stay calm. She was Sade Cole.

He watched her trying to gain control with some satisfaction. He had to meet her before the interview. He could not come on her set and pretend they did not have a past, no matter how brief it was. At least this way, the weirdness would be out of the way of his first TV interview.

Speaking of which.

"I learnt you expressed some reservations about interviewing me. I know better, of course, and didn't buy the excuse of musicians not being up your alley."

She was dumbfounded.

How?

"Not much happens here on ACE that I am not aware of. Especially if it is to do with you." He explained. He rubbed his fingers lightly against his well-defined jaw. The memories of those same hands on her body…

Sade chose wisely to focus on his words.

"Mayowa," she began.

He bent his head slightly sideways. "Few people call me Mayowa these days." He remarked.

She started again, slowly. "Mayowa Fernandez, you will please explain that last line."

"With all pleasure, Sade Cole." He leaned back into the chair. "I own Primetime."

"What? The Braithwaites…"

"I bought majority shares off them eight months ago."

"And this was kept away from the public?"

"You were the public." He announced.

Sade stood up, her eyes blazing and towering over him.

Lynx half smiled to himself. This was the Sade he knew.

"I had a right to know whom I was working for!" she said furiously, pacing around the room.

Who did this? How could anyone drop this kind of bombshell and stay as cool as a cucumber like they did it every day? He probably did!

"Why? So, you could take off to Ittoqqortoormiit?"

He got up too, standing before her, so she stopped

pacing. He was only a couple of inches taller.

"I am not in the habit of running away from my problems." She glared at him. Ittoqqortoormiit? Where in the hell was that?

He gave her a clearly sceptical look. "You will forgive me if I find that just a tad difficult to believe."

She ignored his jibe. He was too close. She could smell him.

"Eight months ago, I was not even here." She pointed out.

"I found out where you were nearly a year ago. Tito did, actually."

"And naturally passed on the message." Her distaste for his sister was evident in her voice.

"Naturally,' Lynx agreed. Tito was not the same person Sade knew.

"Primetime is an excellent business opportunity. ACE is partly personal."

She glanced up at him, understanding fully well what he was saying.

"You head hunted me."

He did not deny it. "You belong on TV. I told you

this. I am right."

The air between them was charged, crackling with electricity. Sade moved away and sat back on the couch. She did not trust her legs to support her anymore, and she did not want to be remembering the intensity of the passion they had shared. The past was a place she no longer went to. *Not voluntarily anyway.* Her eyes settled on the laptop in front of her. His smile leapt off the screen. Was he everywhere in the room?

"I'd say you mean well," she said sarcastically as he went to lean against Tony's desk, putting some more distance between them. "If the word meddling didn't keep popping up in my head."

He dismissed the protest. "Someone has to do a little meddling in your life. From what I hear, you are extremely hardworking, but beyond that, no one really knows you. I told myself the girl just grew into the woman."

"You don't know the first thing about me!"

He raised an eyebrow. "I don't?" He could not stop himself. His look cut at the physical distance between them like a sharp knife. From her eyes to her nose, he lingered on her mouth, slim neck, and breasts. Her nipples became taut against the fabric of her peplum dress. He did not miss it.

She swallowed hard. *That did not mean he knew her.* He was impossible then, and he was impossible now.

"Can we please focus on your interview? There is no point in rehashing the past."

"Yes, to the interview," he said smoothly. "But I'd really like to know what happened back then."

"You want closure." She bit her bottom lip nervously.

His eyes were drawn to the gentle nibbling, and he felt his loin stir with the memory of what she tasted like. He did not want to dwell on how such a little action could evoke those memories.

"An explanation, at the very least," he told her. "You disappeared. You were missing."

Technically, she had not been missing, but she had not, in all honesty, thought he might become incriminated in her "disappearance". She had called Principal Davies from a pay phone later that day to let her know she was not spending the holiday in the boys' quarters. She followed up with a letter weeks later to inform the principal that she was not returning to Queens Grammar.

"I am sorry." She took a deep breath. "For the trouble you got into that day."

"Thank you." He said. "And I am sorry too for my behaviour back then. I later found out things….. yeah, closure will be nice."

She could try and give him the finality he asked for. She could, however, not give him the whole truth.

"But first, I need to make sure your first TV interview is befitting of the legend." She managed a little smile.

The legend you made.

Lynx always thought the man he was today, the name, his musical evolution, and the classic songs that came from a place of deep hurt were all down to this woman.

"I will leave you to it then," Lynx said, moving away from Tony's desk. "But tell me, is it the norm around here to give each other massages?"

"No," Sade responded, a bit flustered.

"Good," Lynx turned away and headed towards the door. "Tell Tony to keep his hands to himself in the future."

He shut the door behind him before she could come up with a suitable retort. She stared into space, trying hard to convince herself he had not just happened again. Except, the smell of him was all around her, encompassing her, making her long for things that had no name.

*****

She left for home from Tony's office. She lived on the Lekki Peninsula. As she drove past the beach from the Victoria Island office of ACE, she wondered about the calm of the ocean, stretching far into the place where the sky met with the sea. How could the world appear so serene when inside, she felt so much anguish? It was unbelievable that Lynx was also now her boss. He was entangled with everything that meant anything in her life. And he did not know how much. He could not be allowed to know how much.

As if on cue, her phone rang.

"Hi." She said.

"Hi, mom. I made something for you."

She smiled. It was a teacher training day, and Femi was home with Teju.

"What is it?"

"It is a secret. Hold on," he went off for a few seconds and returned. "Aunt Teju wants to know if you will be in time for dinner."

"Tell her I am on my way home now."

"Okay, mum, see you soon!"

*****

Half an hour later, she drove through the gates onto her driveway. Femi ran out of the house and threw himself at her. She hugged him fiercely. He was all she truly had.

"Mom," he protested. "You are squashing me."

"Like I can, big man," she said, loosening her hold.

"Where is my present, Nifemi?"

He gave her a secretive smile through his deep-set eyes. Eyes that were so much like his father's.

"You just wait and see."

Sade ruthlessly closed her heart to the voice telling her Femi deserved to know who his father was, and Lynx had a right to know he had fathered a child eight years ago.

Femi was solely hers. All Lynx was, was an unsolicited sperm donor.

Chapter Six

ynx inhaled the early morning tang of the sea deeply, his bare feet digging into the rich sand of the beach as he took a stroll to clear his thoughts. His bodyguard, Declan, was on the periphery of his vision.

His parents had a private beach close to their exclusive Lagos Island mansion. Although he lived mainly in LA, he sometimes retreated here away from the pizzazz of Hollywood. He had last been in Lagos two years ago.

Two years ago, he still had not known what became of Sade.

He remembered looking frantically for her that fateful morning and knocking on the principal's door, adjacent to the boys' quarters, which housed Sade's one-bed apartment. Sade was not there.

The principal was livid when he told her Sade was missing and called security to detain him before calling the police.

That morning, he found out Sade was an orphan.

She had gotten into the exclusive Queens Grammar school on a full scholarship, off the school board, from the parents' charity fund. But she had been said to literally walk into the school with a most impressive academic report from a previous school and threatened suicide if not given a chance at Queens.

He had been terrified. What if she had precisely done that? The thought that she could be gone forever was more than he could conceive. He was released when the principal told the police Sade had called and was alright.

Principal Davies then banned him from the school grounds. He waited in agony for six weeks for the school to resume. But in the new term, Tito called and told him Sade was not returning to Queens. He sent her on an assignment to find out where Sade's previous school had been. Maybe she had gone back there. Tito did not only embarrassingly fail on that mission but had also been humiliated by Principal Davies, who figured out Mayowa was behind it. And out of spite, for there was nothing else to call it, according to Tito, had made Anne, the new editor.

Tito sent him the term magazine once it came out the second week of the new term. He repeatedly read Sade's well-written interview of him and felt both pleasure and pain in nearly equal amounts.

Where was she?

Why did she leave?

Who had she gone to?

He stopped socialising, stopped singing, and fell into depression and self-harm. It was the lowest period in his life, and the only time he had his heart broken.

He looked at the faint scars on his knuckles where he had injured himself from hitting the walls in his bedroom none stop, whilst willing the physical to take away the emotional pains gnawing deep inside. His terrified parents had kept a suicide vigil over him.

Back from school after the final term, Tito could not believe what he had become. He mostly ignored her and sometimes shouted at her. She was part of the problem. She was the torment Sade faced whilst in Queens Grammar. Tito was a mean person. Sade had explicitly asked him not to tell Tito about her. So, it had to be, at least partly, Tito's fault Sade did not return. Who in their sane minds would put up with such a vile human being?

Tito broke down in tears the times he screamed at her.

"I did not know she was an orphan," she had shouted back.

"You do not have to know anything to be a decent person!"

Deciding she had had enough, their mother had dragged them both to America.

And had them in therapy: him, more than Tito.

It was, therefore, ironic that Tito had found Sade first. She had read Sade's piece on human trafficking and the Italian connection over breakfast at their parents' one morning while vacationing in Lagos. She had choked on her meal when she saw the writer's name. *Sade Cole.* Tito had no doubt it had to be her.

After confirming it was indeed *the Sade* via a bit of detective work involving some surveillance work at the newspaper house, her next ordeal was letting him know. She was not sure of the right thing to do. Sade Cole was well and thriving. No one had ruined anyone's life after all.

She finally dropped the news casually into one of their phone conversations, in a by-the-way-guess-who-I saw-in-Lagos manner, hoping he would eventually be at peace where Sade was concerned, and that would be the end of the whole saga. Tito was wrong. He needed more than peace.

He was incapable of giving more of himself to a woman than physical intimacy. She had damaged something in him. He had healed in many ways and had drawn from the pain she inflicted to steer the course of his career and write great songs.

He started out watching her shows to see what it was about her that did this to him. Perhaps, seeing her repeatedly, albeit on a TV screen, might completely heal him of her. Instead, her shows had turned into his guilty pleasure. The years had been very kind to her. She had grown into this stunning woman with heaps of self-confidence, and when she smiled at the cameras, she evoked memories of a night of deep emotional and physical connection—the type he had not had since.

He had pushed for this interview to the surprise of

his management team. He did not owe anyone the reason why. He needed to see Sade again. He needed to look her in the eyes and feel nothing before he could truly move on. He needed to see she was only a human and bled like everyone else.

So far, he had not quite achieved that. He had a girlfriend who loved him, and Michelle deserved a man who could return her love. She knew about his emotional wounds, which his previous girlfriends did not. She wanted Sade demystified so he could move on. And she believed he could grow to love her as he had once loved this schoolgirl. They had met through mutual friends in Hollywood and hit it off almost immediately.

Michelle was a blond beauty, a classical pianist who could hold her own against any woman.

Lynx sighed as he turned back to head home and broke into a jog. The thing was, Sade was not just any woman. She was a conundrum.

*****

Sade's set consisted of a centre stage low round

table, across which she sat from her guests. The studio had a backdrop of brightly coloured panels. Lynx sported a light brown short sleeve snug-fitting cotton-jersey top with dark blue jeans. He had a single gold chain around his neck and remained as easy on the eyes as ever.

Although it was his first TV interview, he was naturally at home with the stage, cameras, and spotlights.

He cracked a few jokes with makeup as they did their final touches and with the camera crew as well.

Sade found he was still as easy to interview as he had been years earlier.

He described his journey into music at a young age, his early inspirations, moving from pop to Afrobeats, and the hiatus in the middle place, the period he had gone to Yale to complete his degree in music and picked up another language along the way. He had come back, drawing on the culture of his African roots, learning from and working with other artistes across the continent. It was fitting that Afrobeats was now taking the world by storm. He talked about his journey into the genre, which, although he had always loved, had taken a particular person in his past to make him see how he fitted into it.

Sade did not even bat an eyelash at this. She expected he would allude to her at some point in his musical journey and was mentally prepared.

She asked questions about the upcoming afrobeats music festival. His eyes lit up as he discussed joining the project and working with other stars. He shared anecdotes about some of the other artistes, some of whom were good friends of his. She found herself laughing, and he found himself laughing with her. On that set, easily, it felt like she had only interviewed him nine days earlier for the school term magazine.

They talked about his Grammy awards and prior multiple nominations. It was great, the recognition, he acknowledged, but Afrobeats as a genre deserved all the honours. The special person who made him see himself in the genre would always have his gratitude, he said, his eyes holding hers steady.

She felt bound to dig into this at this second mention. That was what a journalist would do.

"I think I speak for everyone watching this, that our interest is naturally piqued about this special one. Anyone, we know?"

He chuckled, a touch of mischief in his eyes. "They are very private. Maybe one day, if they feel comfortable enough to come into the limelight, I can share them with the world."

At that moment, she felt everything would be alright in the end. Her eyes said thank you. He smiled back a "You're welcome."

They moved on to other things he enjoyed doing, and he shared the part of him that was also a businessman. He caught her off guard when he mentioned he was a benefactor to several orphanages. He shared his strong belief about money not being an end, but a means to an end, and that end should be the betterment of humanity. He discussed being biracial but felt blessed to be able to embrace his identity than struggle with it.

She ventured into his personal life and Michelle Parker, his pianist girlfriend.

He described her as being a rare find in Hollywood,

a genuinely true person.

"Wedding bells?" She asked.

He laughed. "Not at the moment, but we will see."

In the future, surely, Sade thought sourly but with a bright smile on her face.

She had no inkling of the unrest in his mind even as he spoke of his girlfriend.

Sade wore an asymmetric red cold shoulder dress that fell just below her knees on a gold sandal. He noticed her hair was also parted asymmetrically and obscured her earrings. A choker hugged her graceful neck. She crossed her long legs. He could not help but notice how flawless her skin was. She had indeed grown more beautiful over the years. The picture-perfect image of his first love. She would always be that -nothing anyone could do about it.

Mayowa had learnt to be brutally honest with himself at a young age. And at that moment on her set, he wondered if he would ever be able to look at her and feel nothing. Maybe he just needed to acknowledge that and learn to leave with it. Nine years ago, he had fallen in love at first sight. Today, he was willing to concede he remained attracted to her. What was he going to do about it? Not a damned thing!

Michelle was safety. Sade was the most dangerous woman on the planet. At least to him.

He would call Michelle the moment he got back home. She was his haven.

Sade thanked him for coming on to her show and walked him off the set once the cameras were off.

He responded equally politely, said he would see her around, and left.

*****

Later that night, he called Michelle. It was about lunchtime in LA.

"Hi, baby." He smiled at ease on the phone. He lay sprawled on the bed.

"Hi love, how are you?"

He could picture her on the balcony of her Malibu home, overlooking the beautiful clear Pacific Ocean, in a bra top and sarong, polishing off a meal of salmon dressed in champagne.

"I am good, babes. Miss me?"

"Terribly," she laughed. "How was the big interview? When do I see it?"

"It was perfect, actually. The show is aired a day after the recording, so tomorrow."

"Okay." He heard her draw in a deep breath, "can we address the big elephant in the metaphoric room?"

"Now?"

He could almost see the nod.

"Yep, sweetheart. How is she?"

One of the things he had first liked about Michelle was her straightforwardness. She did not keep anyone guessing how she felt about anything. There was no hidden agenda. You always knew where you stood with her.

Mayowa closed his eyes. "She is fine. Better than that, she's done well for herself."

He heard her sipping a drink.

"And you, how are you? How was it seeing her again after such a long time?"

"The truth?"

"I expect nothing less."

"It was a bit shocking, to be honest."

"Why is that?"

He rolled onto one side of the bed. "It's just how fine she is. What happened back then didn't even touch her."

"And you resent her for this?"

He groaned. "Am I a bad person?"

"Not at all. You spent months in therapy. That is understandable. But beyond that, is there a part of you that might be a bit resentful because your feelings were unrequited?"

Ouch.

"Does it matter now?" He asked her.

"Exactly." She agreed, but her next statement threw him. "If it does matter now, you need to ask yourself why and see if you can draw a line under it. I hate to say this, but I do think you need to speak to her, one on one, off camera."

He thought so too.

He sat up and put the pillow behind him against the headrest. "I know. I just don't know what I will find."

"How else would you know what was going on in her head then?"

"'God, why are we talking about another woman, Michelle?"

"I will come back to that, Lynx, but first, I will tell you this, and I think you already know it. That seventeen-year-old girl had a lot to deal with way before you came on the scene, and your entry into her life did not change that."

"It was never about me." He said, a regretful note he was unaware of creeping into his voice.

Michelle sighed. "It was never, love. It might sound cliché, but I don't think it was ever personal. She was vulnerable but obviously adept at hiding it."

"I took advantage, Michelle. Of an orphan."

"I think orphans around the world might not be too pleased about you lumping them all in a box labelled victim," Michelle paused for effect. "I do not want to be a victim of unresolved emotions."

"Up until nearly a year ago, Sade was a missing person. At least to me. For eight years. How can anyone resolve the unknown?"

"True," Michell agreed quickly. "But the lost has been found, and it is time for the past to be given a befitting burial. But first, we must be sure that it is dead."

Months and months of therapy, and it still came down to this.

A face-to-face with Sade to discuss not just their past but hers as well.

How likely was that to go down well?

Chapter Seven

ade glowered at her laptop screen. She had hardly got any job done. The past weekend had been agonising for her. She was disturbed when she contemplated Nifemi and what the future held for him. For them both. Mayowa had indicated he wanted closure. From their shared past. He was in blissful oblivion of how much of that past was part of her present and would always be a part of her life.

The question was, what was the point in rocking this boat? Nifemi believed his father was in heaven. That bit was not totally unfounded. What Sade knew of Lynx when Femi, as a two-year-old, first asked where his father was, was that he was in Yale. She had told him his father was in New Haven, and the boy had heard Heaven instead. Easier to go along with.

Sade's lips were tightly sealed on the topic of Femi's paternity. Not even Teju knew.

A knock on the door startled her out of her reverie.

"Come in." She called.

It was Kenny Lawal. Sade was surprised to see

him. He had never been to her office before. She pointed to a seat across from her. He heaved his heavy frame into it.

"Is everything okay?" She asked, one eyebrow up. "Management happy with the Lynx interview?"

"Lynx is management!" he blurted out. He contemplated her non-reaction to this.

"You knew. Was that why you didn't want to interview him?"

Sade shook her head vigorously. "No. I didn't know at the time. He mentioned it when he shocked us all with that visit a few days before his interview."

"About that," Kenny started, and Sade frowned, knowing where this was going.

"Is there something you want to share?"

Not really.

"Primetime asked for you. Now in retrospect, I wonder if it was Lynx asking for you. The man did not do TV interviews and then suddenly did. I thought you were lucky, but it was not luck, was it? You and him…."

Sade stopped him there. "Was the interview good,

Kenny?"

"It was perfect." He conceded.

"I will welcome any feedback on my job here. I really will. What I will not welcome are insinuations about me."

"There will be no insinuations if you just cleared the air."

"There is nothing to clear."

"Isn't there? There is obviously a story here, but I am smart enough to sense my job may be on the line if I look where I have no business looking. For now, this is between me and you and Tony. He is a smart man too. If someone else gets wind of it, they may have no reason not to dig. You should be in front of your own narrative."

Sade developed a headache after he left. She took two tablets of paracetamol and decided to bury her head in the sand for now, of all that troubled her.

Work was always therapeutic.

If she could get around to it! No sooner was her headache settling than her phone rang.

"Hello," she said into the phone with the tiniest hint

of impatience.

"Hi!"

It was Lynx. She nearly dropped the phone. Of course, he would have her number.

"Hey, you okay?"

"I am fine, thanks for asking. Look, I wonder if we could grab lunch today. I have some business in your neighbourhood."

He did not. But he was not going to tell her that. He had given some thought to it. Dinner might be misconstrued, but lunch was business.

Sade contemplated it. She did not want to be seen in public with him. Especially not after the little chat with Kenny that morning.

"It's just lunch to talk. Just talk."

Like just friends.

"I know." She said quietly into the phone. "I am just thinking where."

He laughed. "God! Sade. The grapevine will always be around. They have been around from the beginning of time."

She smiled. "True that. But I need to be in control

of my own narrative."

"Heavens, who have you been talking to? I know a place. You will like it. It's quite private."

They met on the rooftop of an exclusive Ikoyi restaurant. The staff there were not allowed to discuss their clientele, Lynx had assured her over the phone.

They now sat across from each other under a large umbrella canopy that provided some shade from the hot Lagos sun. There was a small rectangular table, on top of which were two large glasses of chillingly cold mixed fruit juice garnished with lime wedges.

They both took sips, carefully studying each other. He was wearing denim shorts and an open-neck dark navy shirt. She wondered silently what sort of business meeting he was coming from. Not that it was her business.

After Sade's interview of him, Mayowa had endured other lines of questioning. Tito wanted to know how Sade reacted to seeing him again. He had mentioned she was still as cool as ever, to which Tito had said she supposed that was Sade. His parents called to ask if the interview had brought up any bad memories for him and even had his therapist calling. He was a bit miffed that they were so intrusive. He had politely told them all to mind their businesses as he was no longer nineteen.

"Ask." Sade now interrupted his thoughts.

The command caught him off guard. His eyes were still feasting on her elegant form, albeit involuntarily. She wore a brown Bardot top on a knee-length black belted pencil skirt. Her neck and shoulders were bare, and those legs... The woman tortured the world with them. As she approached the restaurant, he had watched her, his traitorous heart pounding away. She turned every male head and generated quite a few female stares too.

Oh well.

"What do you want to eat?" He asked instead.

She took another sip. "Not hungry, Lynx."

Neither was he.

"Why did you leave that morning?"

It was his turn to catch her off guard. He did not miss the slight shake of her hand. She glanced at him before staring into the distance, at a point just above his right shoulder.

"You were my first." She stated simply.

"I know." He felt a pit at the bottom of his stomach at the thought of who she had been with after him. Which, apart from being hypocritical, did not make sense given what he was trying to achieve here.

"It scared me," she continued. She turned to hold his gaze. "It scared me to believe everything you were saying—all those words. Especially as in the end, one way or the other, you would leave me anyway, and I would be the one picking up all the pieces. I had picked up too many pieces and could not afford to set myself up for another round. I was barely living as it was. So, I left before you could."

"You thought I would have left you?" He was shocked. Did he not express enough how crazy he was about her?

"People always leave. They don't come back, Lynx. My dad, then mum and my sister all did."

"You have a sister?"

"Did." She corrected him. "She died too. Mother had the choice to live, but no, she could not choose us.

We weren't good enough for her to hang around for."

Mayowa felt a chill run down his spine.

"Sade, did your mum kill herself?"

She shrugged. "In a manner." She looked up into the heavens and then down. "My dad goes to hell for sure, and my sister... I am pretty sure she made heaven. As for mother," she waved her right hand in a fifty-fifty fashion, "who knows? She was in hell here, so I suppose a detour to purgatory before heaven was in order."

Her expression was stone cold, and he understood the need to harden her heart to tell him this part of her life. He looked around him. No, this was the wrong place.

"Please come with me." He stood up and pulled her up without waiting for her response. A bodyguard appeared from nowhere and fell in step with them.

His car was parked underground, and a chauffeur appeared immediately.

"Mayowa," Sade tugged on his arm. "I have to get back to work."

"No, you don't. I own the damn company."

She wanted to protest that he did not own her but, seeing the unexpected anguish on his face, decided against it. Besides, she had promised him closure. The chauffeur was patiently holding the car door for her. She got in quietly and said nothing throughout the drive. Her silence seemed to suit him.

They arrived at a palatial mansion in almost no time. He explained it was his parents' home, and they were currently vacationing in the South of France. He had his own quarters.

His living room was moderate-sized, with an exceptionally plush comfortable sofa. Sade thankfully sank her tired self into it.

He came to sit beside her.

"Do you want a drink? Anything?"

"No." She replied. "What else do you want to know?"

"You were thirteen when you got into Queens Grammar." He stated, and she nodded her agreement. "They were all…." He could not bring himself to say the word.

"All dead, yes."

"How old was your sister?"

"Temilade was seventeen."

God. Only a child. The exact age Sade was when he met her.

"How did she pass?"

"She was murdered. I found her body. I had been out looking for her."

At thirteen.

He felt the blood drain from his face. And watched in horror as she went to that memory, to the place, a place far from him, and to a time, the time that was before him. He watched the facade crumble slowly, and then a tear rolled down. And then some more.

Wiser this time, he let her be. He handed her a pack of tissue, maintaining a barely bearable silence.

"Sorry." She said as the tears ebbed away.

Sorry? He was the sorry one.

"Don't. I… if I had known… God." He covered his face almost as if in shame.

She touched his lower arm briefly. "You didn't know then, but now you know; it was…."

"It was not about me." He finished for her.

She looked at him in puzzlement. "Oh, it was also about you."

"What? What do you mean?"

"About men like you. Like him."

"Like whom?" Mayowa was disconcerted.

"Do you remember the visiting day at Queens Grammar you sent Tito to get me?" She asked him.

"Yes, I do." There was not a moment to do with her that he truly forgot.

"Do you remember the song I taught you?"

"The heart of this prince." He replied.

"Yep, the heart of this prince. That song was my dad's."

"You said you didn't know whose it was."

"I lied."

He felt a little knot in his stomach.

"Your dad was a musician." It was said as a statement. "Who you think deserves to be in hell."

"Oh, he is in hell." She assured him emphatically.

He took both of her hands in his and drew closer to her.

"Look at me, Sade, and tell me you know for a fact

I will end up in hell."

She was flustered. "I cannot say that about you. I don't know…."

"Exactly. You didn't know me. Enough. You never got to know me, but that didn't stop you from lumping me in the same boat as your dad. You pigeon-holed me."

He was not angry with her. How could he be? He just wanted her to see another perspective.

"It was also the only way," she told him, "the only way I could deal with… that situation… how I felt about you at the time."

Mayowa felt a warmth going around in his chest. It was unexpected but not unwelcome.

"How did you feel about me at the time?"

"Fishing?"

He shook his head, dead serious. "It's a need to know. After you disappeared, I spent months in therapy, and that knowledge might have spared me some pain."

"What? You did what?"

"In America. Don't forget that I had no idea what

became of you until nearly a year ago. It was not a nice place to be."

Sade looked down at her hands still in his, closed her eyes briefly, took a deep breath and opened her eyes.

"I was falling in love with you, Mayowa. It was a luxury I could not afford. So, I ran, and I really could not come back."

"You could not come back to me."

She gradually withdrew her hands from his. "No, I couldn't."

"Could you have if I was not Mayowa, the pop star?"

"Maybe I would have. But you…you were too much. In my mind, too much like him, and I could not be like my mother. He destroyed her in the end. I had to save myself before you could wreck my life."

"You were that sure I was going to destroy your life?"

"I was. My father was an unrepentant cheat. He was faithless. He was good-looking and incredibly talented too but was too much into all sorts of depravities to make any great use of it. Celebrities, artistes, stars. You just cannot help yourself when you can have almost anyone you want."

"Let me clear this first stereotype," Lynx said in the most serious tone he could muster. "I will have you know I have never cheated on a woman."

She looked at him, clearly unbelieving.

"A serial monogamist, yes. But a cheat? Never. I would never have cheated on you."

'But you would have dumped me when the next best thing came along,' Sade thought.

Lynx read her thoughts perfectly but chose not to argue the point. *One thing at a time.*

"So, where did you go?" He asked.

"My old neighbourhood." She replied. "Old family friends took me in and made sure I completed my education."

"Like that?"

"A bit more complicated than that, but," she smiled a dazzling smile that took his breath away. "I am here today, ain't I?"

Indeed, she was.

Lynx leaned back into the sofa. She had explained a lot, and a part of him was deliriously happy that she had felt what he felt. The other part wished he had done things differently. That he had built friendship and trust first, but he had only been nineteen. He had not known any better.

He thought about what Michelle had said about why it mattered now. The why needed a full self-introspection. Because from where he sat at that moment, barely able to take his eyes off Sade, feeling the grip she had on his heart like a physical thing, it was silly to think a line existed that could be drawn under what he still felt for her.

He had to talk to Michelle. Face to face.

Chapter Eight

The international afrobeats festival took place the following weekend, which was all her crew talked about during the week.

Tony asked if she was going after all and seemed taken aback when she said no.

"But you and Lynx…."

Sade dragged him to a corner of the studio before he could complete the statement publicly.

"What exactly do you think you know about Lynx and me?"

"You knew each other. The way he barged in and then kicked me out of my own office!"

Sade sighed. "Yeah, I knew him long ago but was shocked like you were when he came in that day."

"I saw…everyone in this studio saw, the way he looked at you at that interview…. do you two have a history?"

"With Lynx? You do realise he is a megastar, right?"

"And you do realise he is only a man, and you are

an extremely attractive woman?"

Sade blinked several times at the unexpected compliment.

"Quite intimidating too," Tony continued. "The three months you have been here, do you have any idea how many times I have tried asking you out and end up inviting you to a group outing instead?"

"I am sorry if I come across as daunting, but I'd rather keep my private life away from work."

"So, you couldn't date a colleague anyway?"

Sade nodded. "No offence."

"Some taken, but it doesn't matter, does it?"

Sade said nothing.

He sighed. "You are the news waiting to break, Sade. Be careful."

Sade watched the music festival on TV with Femi in the comfort of their home that weekend.

Teju had gone to a relative's wedding in Ibadan.

Femi knew some of Lynx's songs, and watching him sing and dance along was heart-wrenching. He sang beautifully like his father. But also like his grandfather too, Sade acknowledged. Femi was the best of them all. He was an innocent beautiful child who was genuinely kind-hearted and selfless. He always made little cards for her and insisted on sharing all his candies with her. His teachers often commented on how well she was raising him, but she knew he was innately a thoughtful boy.

At times, as the years went by, she had caught herself wondering how much of his personality was his father's, but she had also reminded herself of the vile Tito, who, after all, was Femi's biological aunt.

Watching Lynx on TV, his son, now curled up on her lap, exhausted, Sade wondered about the right thing. She had no idea what he would do if he found out about Femi. The thought was truly terrifying. If he went back to LA without much ado, it might not matter at all if she kept her private life, aka Femi, away from the public eye. But Lynx now owned Primetime as well as ACE, which put her firmly in a place where he had access to her easily. At least at work.

He had a girlfriend, Sade told herself firmly. *In LA, where he lived.*

LA would never be on their vacation list.

"Mum?" Femi interrupted her musings.

"Yes, honey."

"Can I go to Dele's birthday party, please?"

Femi was asking for the umpteenth time. Sade was undecided yet. Dele was Femi's classmate, and his parents were socialites. Sade did not particularly want to hobnob with them.

"Let's ask aunt Teju if she will take you when she returns?"

"Why can't you take me, mum?"

Because I am hiding you and me together away from the world.

"I am sorry, I will be working that weekend."

"You never take me anywhere, mum!" Femi sulked.

"That's unfair, Femi. I took you to Disneyland Paris for your birthday."

He laughed and hugged her. "Yes, you did, mum. But when it's my next birthday, can I invite all my friends and have a birthday party too?"

She kissed his head. "Yes, Femi. If that's what you want."

He had never had one with friends over. Birthdays were usually affairs with just the three of them.

Sooner or later, Lynx was bound to find out about his son. It was unfair to rob Femi of a normal childhood to keep his father away from him. It was also unfair to rob Lynx of the opportunity to be in Femi's life if he wanted to be.

Mayowa Fernandez was, after all, not a bad person.

Sade knew what she had to do. She had to talk to him again. She had to tell him.

She only prayed she could wither the storm that was surely coming.

No matter what happened, Femi had to be protected.

****

A few days later, events were taken out of her hands when she learnt Lynx had returned to Los Angeles.

She was hurt that he had not even thought to say goodbye to her.

And when she saw his picture on an internet gossip magazine dining out with Michelle, his hand on the small of her back, she realised Lagos was his holiday and LA was home.

She resented that he had breezed in to rock her neatly organised life. She hated that she was hurting and that he had made her doubt she was doing the right thing by Femi.

She looked at her schedule and luckily realised taking a few days off to reset was doable.

She needed to reconnect back to herself. Find Sade Cole again.

The Sade Cole who was the strongest person she knew.

*****

"So, you fled back here, Lynx?" Michelle asked, noticing how tense he was.

The matter was comical if her heart was not slowly breaking into pieces.

They were dining at the Nobu Malibu. The food was as exquisite as always, but, on this occasion, Lynx could hardly taste it. And Michelle barely touched her food as well.

"I needed the distance to clear my head."

"Or to see and compare me to her?"

"That is not fair, Michelle."

Michelle took a sip of wine. "I saw her."

Lynx looked at her quizzically. "The interview?"

"Yeah. She is a very beautiful woman, Lynx."

Lynx said nothing to the announcement of the obvious.

"I don't want to lose you, Lynx." Michelle rubbed her forehead. "Lord, in retrospect, asking you to meet with her was a terrible idea!"

Lynx shuttered his emotions. "You had the right idea, Michelle. And you are also right not to want a man with feelings for another woman."

Michelle tilted her head to one side. "I…. I thought……. hoped that you would realise she wasn't all that and that your mind made her out to be something more because of all that mystery that surrounded her and how it all ended with her disappearance."

"What I went through was real." Lynx did not want to hurt her, but the truth had to be said. "I didn't self-harm nor go to therapy for the fun of it."

"I am sorry," Michelle apologised. "I didn't mean to disparage what was a difficult time in your life."

Lynx took hold of both of her hands. "And I am sorry. That I am not the man you had hoped I would be."

"Don't be," Michelle said. "You never lied about this part of you. The heart wants what the heart wants. As much as it is killing me to say this, and even though I hate her so much, you deserve this epic love of yours. You are a good man."

She raised his knuckles to her lips and kissed them. "Take the time you need to clear your head, go back to her, and please don't come back to America needing therapy again."

✳✳✳✳✳

A few days later, Lynx called Sade to hear her voice, to feel his heart beating wildly again as only she could make it, but his calls did not go through.

He got through to Kenny at ACE, who told him Sade had suddenly taken a few days off.

He had a nearly overwhelming sense of Déjà vu but forced himself to remain calm. What was she up to now? Only Sade could mess around with his head like this. The grip she had on him messed around with time itself. In nine years, he finally made sense of himself to himself. Sade explained him. He was still in love with her. How did she feel about him now?

There was only one way to find out, but he was sure she was not immune to him. She was not, nine years ago, by her own admission, and she was not now either. He had seen her hands shake around him, her nipples hardening, and her breath quickening at his proximity.

He made a few phone calls, first to his manager and then to his PA.

He called Tito next. She lived in New York and worked there as a corporate lawyer. Tito worked hard, played hard, and was always in a hurry.

She answered his call breathlessly.

"Hi, Mayowa! Make it quick. Learnt you were

back in town by the way from the paparazzi."

"Hi, you too! Call me when you can chat, will you?"

"Sure, I was thinking of swinging by next weekend and having dinner with you and Michelle."

"Can't do. I am on my way back to Lagos."

"Why? What's happening in Lagos?"

"Sade."

The silence on the other end was almost palpable, and the sound of a chair being drawn announced Tito felt the need to sit down for this.

"Are you sure, Mayowa?"

"I have never been more certain of anything else in my life. I just wanted to let you know I won't be in town for a while."

"How long is a while?"

"For as long as it takes."

"And Michelle?"

"We are over."

"Shit." Tito cursed.

"Michelle is a good person but deserves better than me."

"No kidding. But it's always been Sade."

"Yes, Tito. It has always been Sade."

"I am sure you know what you are doing. Let me know if there's any way I can help."

"About that… what do you suppose are the legal consequences of digging around for your employee's home address for personal reasons?"

"You are going to stalk her?" Tito let out a stream of expletives.

*****

It was Dele Akande's birthday party that Saturday and Femi was super excited. Although he had not been to Dele's home before, he regurgitated all his peers had told him of the house.

"Dele's house is big, mum. Ginormous. They have a big swimming pool."

"I am sure they do," Sade said as she neatly wrapped the present and handed it to him.

The birthday was superhero-themed, and Femi was a big fan of Thor. He proudly wielded his hammer in one hand and took the present off her with the other.

Teju, who enjoyed the Lagos social scene more than she cared to let on, was happy to take him.

Sade waved them off, watching Teju's range rover disappear through the gates. She had been at home the past few days and mainly lazed around for the first two, enjoying the art of doing nothing tangible. However, on day three, she had started playing around with some materials that she was sure Tony and Kenny would be pleased with. Tony was convinced he had something to do with her sudden need to take a few days off. He texted an apology for stepping out of line, to which she had replied it had nothing to do with him.

Keen to do some cooking while she had the house to herself, she donned an apron, took some beef from the freezer to thaw and pulled vegetables from the fridge to chop up.

She was startled when the doorbell rang. She was not expecting Teju and Femi back for another few hours. She wondered what it was they forgot.

She opened the door and instantly froze.

Lynx on her doorstep. In dark sunglasses and a baseball cap, that did not particularly do a good job of hiding his identity. She did not notice her hyperexcitable neighbour who had let him in through the gates. Nor did she see his tinted windowed Land cruiser and his bodyguard close by.

Her whole world narrowed down to one man and the thought of the son that he had probably just gone past on the road. Her vision tunnelled and then blurred off.

"Sade!" was the last thing she heard before her knees gave way.

He had envisioned different ways she might react to him showing up uninvited on her doorstep, but this was not one of them.

He had imagined surprise, yes, and anger even. He was even prepared for the very unpleasant scenario that she lived with a man. He knew she was single, but that did not mean she was not dating.

But a faint?

Maybe she was ill; the morbid thought occurred to him. Perhaps that was why she was taking time off work in the first place.

He caught her fall and carried her through the half-opened door into her living room, his attention solely on her. His bodyguard followed him in, and so did the neighbour who, thank God, announced himself as a medical doctor and advised Lynx to lay her down on the couch. She groaned only a few moments after he did.

"Sade," he whispered, realising she was coming to.

"I will go get some water." The doctor said and hurried along.

Lynx was leaning over her when Sade came fully to. She tried to get up.

"No, Sade," he gently pushed back. "The doctor said you must lie down. He said something about vasovagal."

Lynx smiled his roguish boyish smile. "He said you were too excited to see me. Is that true?" He caressed her hair and kissed her forehead, ignoring his bodyguard. The doctor returned with a big jug of water and a glass cup.

Sade sat up slightly and gulped down the whole cup.

Lynx surely would be the death of her.

"Thanks, doc. I am fine now."

"Glad to be of some help," the doctor, Segun, said. "Call me if you need me."

"Will do." She muttered.

Lynx thanked him and said he hoped to see him again, to which the doctor gushed and left.

Sade looked up at him, smiling happily at her, and then noticed his bodyguard staring at the wall. She nearly fainted back again. She wished she could faint back again.

The wall.

With Femi's picture.

Sade's hands flew to her mouth to stifle a cry. Confused, Lynx turned around to follow the direction of her gaze to his bodyguard and then the wall.

And the picture on the wall.

Of a boy.

Lynx stood up slowly from where he had been crouching next to her. He walked to the wall and stared at the picture for what seemed like an eternity.

"Mayowa," Sade started, unsure what she would say next. Femi was the split image of his father, a darker shade, but the eyes, the smile, and the jawline were unmistakable.

Mayowa held up a hand.

"How old is he?"

Sade let out a little sob.

"How old, Sade?"

"He is eight." She blurted out.

"He's...."

Sade nodded miserably behind him. Not that he could see her. She watched him touch the picture of their son gently, in disbelief. In shock.

"Say it, Sade." He said quietly.

She had never heard him that way before. He sounded like he was at the last stop before a complete meltdown. Sade glanced nervously at the bodyguard, who moved his own body and, not so subtly, planted himself between the two.

Lynx, turning around slightly, noticed this and asked his bodyguard to leave, still in that quiet voice that fooled no one.

"I am sorry, Lynx. I can't do that."

Sade got up. This was her mess.

"He's yours, Mayowa. I am sorry." She said slowly.

He turned back at her and looked at her as if she were a stranger. She lived with a male quite rightly. His son!

"How could you, Sade?" His voice dripped with contempt. "How dare you?"

She said nothing. She could take his wrath. She was thankful Femi was not at home at this moment.

"You lied to me! He was why you didn't come back, wasn't he? You got pregnant with my child! Couldn't you tell me? I would have taken care of you, both of you!"

Sade remained silent.

"You decided I was the same as your miserable daddy, didn't you?"

Sade had no conscious thought before flying in Lynx's direction. His bodyguard stopped her in mid-flight.

"Ma'am, please. Keep your distance."

Lynx did not even move a muscle. "Where is he?"

Sade did not reply.

"What is his name?"

"Nifemi." She said and wandered over to the window to keep the requested distance between them.

"Love me." Lynx translated smoothly. His mouth twisted bitterly. "Ironic that."

He turned his attention back to the pictures on the wall. Sade on the Seine with his child. They looked happy. He noticed the picture of an older woman and pointed to it.

"Who is that?"

"Aunt Teju."

"You have an aunt?"

She sighed, feeling the fight ebbing away from her. "No, she took me in after… after Queens Grammar…."

"The family friend," Lynx stated. "She looked after the pregnant you, right?"

Sade nodded. "And she looked after Femi when I went back to school. She sorted everything. She… she gave me back my life…."

Lynx stiffened. He had not deliberately set out to destroy her life.

"Where is she?"

"We live together. She is family now."

Lynx turned back to her. "So, she is the one out with him. Where did they go?"

Sade felt somehow caught out.

"It doesn't matter if you tell me where he is now or not. Rest assured that I am not leaving until I meet my child. What did you tell him about me anyway?"

Sade glanced nervously at the bodyguard again. All these dirty linens were hanging out in public!

"He… he thinks…believes you died."

Chapter Nine

Lynx did not think it was possible to become more outraged, but Sade was the gift that kept giving.

"You told him I died?"

"Not exactly." She defended delicately.

"Please clear this fog in my mind. How?"

"You were in Yale at the time he asked about you. I said you were in New Haven, and he thought I said you were in heaven."

It was genuinely the most ridiculous thing he had ever heard. And cruel.

What mother did this to her child?

Lynx reached into his pocket and took out his phone. He called Tito. It was about nine in the morning in New York.

"Hey, bro. How's operation Sade going?"

"Terrible." His voice was ragged, his breathing uneven.

"Calm down, Mayowa. What's happened?"

"You will not believe why she never returned to

Queens Grammar."

Sade hearing his side of the conversation, raised an eyebrow nearly into her hairline.

She left the windowsill and walked towards him.

"Who are you talking to?" She shouted at him.

"Gosh, is that Sade?" Tito asked, anxiety creeping into her voice. Even across the thousands of miles, Tito felt the trepidation of all their shared past. "What is going on there, Lynx?"

"She was pregnant, Tito. With my son."

"What!" Tito screamed into the phone.

"Who are you talking to, Lynx?" Sade repeated herself.

"Tito," he replied tersely. "She is a cutthroat lawyer these days."

"Don't you dare, Mayowa," Tito warned him. "Don't threaten her with me. You know our history."

"Exactly."

"Oh God! Now, it all makes sense. Of course, she couldn't return to school." Tito groaned. "Why didn't we consider that possibility? Have you met your son?"

"No. She was not going to tell me about him. I

found out accidentally today, but even now, she wouldn't tell me where he is."

"Can you send your PJ for me? I am coming over."

"Will do. See you soon."

Sade patiently listened to the several other calls he made. She figured out Tito was coming over, and his parents were cutting short their holiday in the South of France. She was acutely aware that even as he made his calls, his eyes never really left her. He monitored her movements, and she knew he was bidding his time until Femi and Teju returned. Knowing they would return at some point. What was he going to do once he met his son? She knew as she breathed that she could not lose her child.

Once he was done with his calls, he came to sit on the sofa, keeping her directly in his line of vision. She sat directly opposite him to show she was not up to any mischief.

"Would you both like a drink?" She offered to break the ensuing terrible silence.

The distrust in his eyes was unmistakable.

"No, we do not." He spoke on behalf of his

bodyguard, who Sade actually thought could do with one!

"Femi is at a friend's birthday party. Aunt Teju took him."

Lynx believed this and was also beginning to think this Teju was more of a mother to his son. And clearly a significant person in his life.

"Can we talk in private?" Sade asked. "No offence to…"

"Declan." Lynx's bodyguard supplied.

"No offence to Declan, before Femi returns from the party."

Lynx looked at Declan. "Sure." He agreed. Declan hesitated for a few seconds, then, deciding the energy in the room appeared calmer, nodded his head.

"I will be right outside the door." He said, almost as a warning to both.

Sade smiled slightly. Lynx did not find anything funny.

It was a relief that it was now out of her hands, and she no longer had to battle her conscience about doing the right thing. She felt a weight lifted off her shoulders while at the same time was terrified of what his next actions would be, as he appeared to be already considering his legal options.

But more importantly, she worried about her son. How do you tell an eight-year-old that his father was not only not dead but a megastar that he had known of all along?

"I am sorry, Lynx. Truly sorry." She began.

He did not reply to this.

"Please, you have to believe me."

"I don't have to do any such thing, Sade."

"I should have told you. And I was going to tell you."

"When exactly? You could easily have nine years ago. You could have at any point in the last nine years if you truly wanted to. You could have told me the first time I came to ACE. What about when we talked one-to-one about what happened nine years ago? I cannot even imagine how you could sit in front of me on multiple occasions and deny me the knowledge that I have a child!"

"I was going to after we talked, but you left for

America. You didn't even say goodbye."

"Now, it is my fault."

"What I am saying, Lynx, please hear me, is that I am sorry." Sade got up and went to sit next to him.

The fury in his eyes was terrifying, and she felt he would never forgive her.

"Why? It's all I wanna know. Why didn't you come to me the moment you knew you were pregnant?"

She reached for his hand, expecting him to push her away at any moment. She felt a little hope when he did not.

"I became quite sick very early on in the pregnancy, just as the holidays were ending. It's called hyperemesis. For three months, I was bedbound. Not much food or drink stayed down. No medicine seemed to work. Aunt Teju, bless her, tried everything she was told should work. I was in and out of the hospital for drips to hydrate me. I lost weight. I was malnourished and a shell of myself, a shell filled with much shame and rock bottom disappointment in myself. Return was the last thing I could do."

She paused to let the image sink in.

"If you'd returned," Lynx moved slightly on the sofa so he could fully face her. "I would have looked after you. My child is my responsibility, Sade. You were both my responsibility. I was broken after you left, but that was nothing compared to what you went through." He finished bitterly, but his voice had softened a bit.

"Let's go down that path, shall we?" Sade tilted her head to one side. "Do you not think it would have been too much for you to take on as a twenty-year-old pop star, and you would eventually have resented me? At some point, wouldn't you have felt trapped and yearned for freedom? And taken our child as the courts would probably decide he was better off with your more stable family. I would have lost my child, my dignity, and everything I had sworn I would never allow a mortal to take away from me."

"I would not have abandoned you!" He half shouted and then turned the dial down as they heard Declan coughing pointedly just outside the door. "We would have grown together and raised our child together."

Sade sighed sadly, not convinced. "It's the road taken and the road not taken. As that pregnant seventeen-year-old, what I saw of my future, based on my past, terrified me. When we met, I was a broken child, just about holding it together. Step into my shoes for a second, and please see what I saw."

She caressed the back of his hand. And felt the expected electricity between them. His fingers wavered slightly, and she knew he felt it too.

"In all of these, believe me, I was going to tell you just before I found out you had returned to LA."

Lynx looked at the hand caressing his and felt his hands shaky of their own accord. He looked away from the tell-tale sign of his weakness and his gaze locked with hers. And immediately felt himself falling and drowning in the sadness in her deep brown eyes. His were filled with regrets about all that had happened and the powerlessness to change the past.

"I am sorry, Lynx," Sade whispered, her eyes conveying her own regrets more than any words could. He nodded, acknowledging the apologies for the first time. He couldn't take his eyes off her mesmerising eyes, her excruciatingly beautiful face, those lips… He inhaled sharply. He was finished.

Without taking his eyes off her, he raised his voice ever so slightly to tell Declan he needed some privacy and asked him to go get some lunch with the chauffeur. They heard Declan physically retreating from the door.

Lynx pulled her closer, and his mouth descended to capture hers. The line was thin between anger and desire, and passion won easily.

Sweet.

Torture.

Heaven.

His tongue delved inside her mouth, seeking and wildly probing. He untied the apron around her waist and slipped it over her head. His hands went under her top, unfastened her bra, and cupped both breasts. She moaned into his mouth. She tingled in places she didn't know she had places. And was losing control…. rapidly.

"Wait," she said breathlessly.

He paused and lifted one eyebrow in a silent

enquiry, his expression tormented.

"You and Michelle?"

"Michelle and I are over." He replied and added in a soft tone. "I don't cheat. Is there anything else bothering you?"

She shook her head slowly.

"I am dying here. Please tell me you want me too." He said shakily.

"I want you." She told him and pulled him back to her.

She could not resist him. Had never been able to resist him. She was not interested in resisting him. Her hands went under his shirt, caressing his chest, the little hairs. She touched a nipple, and she heard him groan in pleasure. She stroked his chest muscles and slipped a hand down his lean, muscular abdomen, and groin. He groaned again and pulled away momentarily to carry her off the couch.

"Where is your bedroom?" He asked harshly.

Lynx wanted her so badly. He threw her on the king-sized bed, over the soft sheets, and continued his assault on her senses. He kissed her as he had in many dreams, deeply, passionately, and was rewarded with how she trembled and moaned in his arms. He fondled her perky breasts, kissed them, and loved all of her, giving her as much pleasure as he received. He touched every part of her body, felt how wet she was for him, how much she wanted him too.

He donned protection as quickly as he could and went slowly into her at first, stroked her gently, and as he lost restraint, thrust faster and harder into her. She held on tight to him, digging into his back, moving to meet his pace, her hands all over his back, on his buttocks, drawing him deeper into her.

They both climaxed simultaneously, clinging to each other for dear life.

And yet he had not had enough. Neither had she. He rolled onto his back and tossed her over him so she was astride him, and he pushed himself up into her. Sade quivered at the sheer sensation. She bent down to kiss him again while he fondled her breasts. She rode him to another unbelievable height. Finally, exhausted, they both collapsed onto the bed.

Hungry.

He followed her to the kitchen and watched as she prepared a quick meal of boiled yam and scrambled eggs with vegetables. She wore a bra top and shorts that showed off her long legs and flawless skin. He had only his jeans on, and Sade struggled to keep her eyes off him as she prepared their meal.

Lynx wolfed his down and helped wash the dishes. As she put the last plate out to dry, he sneaked up behind her, pushed her gently against the worktop, and pulled down her shorts and panties in one motion. She felt his groin against her bottom. She had not even seen him pull down his jeans. She shivered in anticipation. He kissed the nape of her neck, turned her mouth to meet his open one, and thrust inside her from behind, his strong hands supporting her waist. Sade felt more alive at that moment than she ever had. He was so sweet, so giving, and a generous lover.

Sade climaxed and fell backwards into his arms seconds before he gripped her waist even tighter, dug himself entirely into her, and gave a big shudder.

She turned slowly in his arms to face him and put a hand on his powerful chest.

"What is this, this thing always boiling between us?"

"What it's always been." He monitored the slight confusion in her eyes. "We are attracted to each other. You fight it. I cannot."

"I used to think of it as an animal. An animal I ought to kill."

Lynx chuckled. "Please let our animal live."

"What happened with you and Michelle?" She asked, thinking of the serial monogamist.

"You happened. We were over the moment I saw you again. It just took me a while to consciously come to that truth. It is not right that Michelle and I continue living a lie."

Realisation dawned on her. "You went back to LA to talk to her and came back…."

"I came back to you and for you." He said.

"You came back to my deception. To this massive secret."

He gripped her shoulders, nearly inflicting pain.

"Yes, it is life-changing, and yes, it will take a little getting used to, but it is not a deal breaker. All I need is the truth from you moving forwards. No more lies. Nothing but the truth. Can you do that?"

"Yes, I can." Sade was overwhelmed by his confessions and that he had just forgiven her the almost unforgivable.

"If I hadn't come here today, would you have found a way to tell me about our son? Even though I had gone back to LA?" He asked her.

"After our talk at your parents'," she replied, "I had decided that you needed to know. I was hurt that you went back to LA without as much as a goodbye because you got your closure. That's why I took some days off work. But I would have found the courage to tell you, Lynx, for both of your sakes and then bear the consequences."

He relaxed his hold and stroked her shoulder. He believed her. And she had felt hurt by him, which meant she cared.

"I must ask. Is there someone else? Are you seeing anyone?"

Sade scowled at him. "You think I just cheated on someone with you?"

"I don't think so, Sade." Not from everything he now knew about her.

"No, I am not seeing anyone. Femi is the only man in my life."

"You will always have me in your life too."

"I know," she sighed. He was referring to the son they shared, of course. From the moment he had walked into her life, Sade thought, Mayowa had never really left.

He read her mind and locked his hands behind her waist to keep her encircled in his arms. They would be on the same page this time.

"Sade," he said softly. "As I said before, I came back to you. To ask that you be mine. To try again in this lifetime."

"You are asking me to date you," Sade said as a statement, but he treated it as a question.

"Yes, I am asking you to date me. Formally. Be mine."

She looked away from him, unable to meet his eyes lest he saw the effects he was having on her. She had never wanted anything as much as she wanted him, which gave him enormous power over her.

"What is dating you like, Lynx?"

"Whatever we want it to be." He moved his head sideways, seeking to regain eye contact. "The only way I can prove myself to you is if you let me prove me to you. I am sorry for what I said about your dad before. You confided in me, and I know how difficult it is for you to open up to anyone. I used it against you, and I am ashamed of that. It will never happen again. But I am not him. Do not project him onto me."

"I am Sade Cole. I am my own person, Lynx."

"That is the person I want to be with."

She turned back to look him in the eyes. "If I date you, my life will not be subject to your whims and caprices."

God. Her father had really done a number. If anyone needed therapy, it was this love of his. But one thing at a time.

"You will never be, Sade."

"If you ever cheat on me...."

"I will never cheat on you. I do not cheat."

The serial monogamist.

"If you want to write a list of demands," he told her, "in a legal document, set out terms and conditions; I will happily sign it. Sade, I am crazy about you."

She chuckled, and he visibly relaxed.

"Well, I did say that you could ask in my next life."

He smiled at the memory. "Yes, you did. So…."

She rose on tiptoes and kissed his lips.

"What does that mean? You have to say it, Sade. I speak few languages, but woman isn't one of them."

She smiled widely at him. "I am yours."

"Say it again." He pulled her tighter, licking her bottom lip with his tongue.

"I said I will be yours." She repeated. "Gosh, you know how to convince a woman."

He could not tell her she was the only woman he had ever needed to convince to be with him. He kissed her fiercely, his hands back on her breasts, stroking her nipples. He was rudely interrupted by the ringing of her mobile phone.

"Ignore them," he told her huskily. "I'd really like to make love to my woman. Officially this time."

"It's probably aunt Teju. They might be on their

way back, Lynx."

She was right.

"They are coming back," Sade told him in some panic. "Even with some traffic, they should be back in thirty minutes."

"A lot could happen in thirty." He whispered into her ear.

She gave him a little jab in the side. "Get dressed. You are about to meet your son."

"Yes, ma'am." He said in a mocking tone to disguise a sudden sense of apprehension. He did as she asked, and they withdrew back to the living room once they were fully clothed. She went to hover by the door. He held her from behind, his chin atop her head.

He only relaxed his hold when they heard a car driving into the compound. She parted the curtains and peeped through.

"It's them." She announced.

She felt Lynx stiffen.

"It will be alright." She told him more calmly than she felt inside. "Let me."

Sade opened the door and stepped out of the living

room.

Femi leapt out of the range rover as soon as it was parked, eager to share his day and the party souvenirs with her.

"Mum, look what I got!" He shouted and ran to hug her. Teju got out of the car leisurely, carrying more bags of goodies.

"You should have been there, Sade. You would not believe the people I met today!"

Sade had an idea but could not dwell on this, given the critical mission at hand.

She gently kissed Femi on the forehead.

"I have a surprise for you, Nifemi."

Femi held her hand and swung it back and forth.

"What is it, mum?"

"Inside. I want you to meet someone."

She met Teju's questioning look over his head. "You too, auntie."

Femi dragged his mum towards the door. "Come on, mum!"

They rarely had visitors in their home, and it was a novelty for Femi that there was someone to be met today.

Sade held his little hand, and they both stepped into the living room, with Teju closely behind.

Lynx was pacing in the room. He spun around when he heard the door opening, and his son leapt into the room.

"Femi," Sade began.

"Mum!" Femi screamed, abruptly letting go of his mother's hand. "Is that Lynx?"

"Yes, that is Lynx. Mayowa... Lynx meet…Femi and this is aunt Teju."

For the life of him, Lynx could not speak at that very second. There was a lump the size of an apple in his throat.

Father and son were staring at each other. Nearly a mirror image of each other.

His son.

He crouched low and took hold of his son's hand. "Very nice to meet you, Femi." He managed to croak out.

He respectfully dipped his head at Teju. "And you too, aunt Teju."

Teju stared at him. "Sade, the Lynx?"

"Yes, auntie," Sade replied nervously. Surely Teju would put it all together.

"Woo! That is one big shocker. Sade didn't tell us you are friends."

"Lynx!" Femi shouted again. "In my house! I will tell all my friends, mum!"

Lynx laughed, feeling the tension leaving his body at the innocence of childhood.

"Tell you what, Femi, the honour is all mine, and I can't wait to tell everyone about you too." He pulled the boy into his embrace tightly. Tears rolled down his cheeks as he wept silently over his son's head. He mouthed sorry to Sade. Her eyes also filled with tears, which rolled down her cheeks uncontrollably. Teju took in the scene, looked at the man and the boy, and her hands flew to her mouth. She let out a strangled sound. Sade took hold of her arm and quickly led her away from the lounge through the dining room into the kitchen.

"Is he…is he Femi's father?"

Sade nodded, unable to speak.

"All these years… Sade… it was Lynx. Lynx! Oh my God. I need to sit down." Teju drew a seat at the kitchen island.

"I am sorry. I just could never talk about him."

"Even to me? I always feared the worst, like someone raped you."

Sade winced. "God, no, he didn't. We met when I was at Queens Grammar. His sister was my classmate."

"God…Sade… And you just recently interviewed him too. Did he know?"

She shook her head. "No, he only just found out today. He turned up here to surprise me and happened on Femi's picture. The one in the living room."

"Lord have mercy! You weren't going to tell him. And he is not even mad at you!"

"Oh, but he was. Pretty mad. His bodyguard had to intervene."

Teju looked around as if the said bodyguard was hiding somewhere about in the kitchen.

"Declan is gone. Lynx asked him to leave."

"What's going to happen now, Sade? Do you think

he will take Femi away from us?"

"He can't. I mean, he doesn't want to."

Sade put her hands together. "There is something else you should know."

"What? More surprises?"

"He has asked me to be with him. He wants us to be together. That's why he came here today in the first place. I said yes."

"And you want to be with him?"

Sade nodded. "I do. I know it's all very sudden in a manner, but every time I am around him, I become something more. I feel more alive."

Sade sat down too and held her head in between her hands. "Oh, aunt Teju. I am crazy about him. I have always been."

Teju smiled. "He does come across as a nice person. I like him. But what a day you have had!"

"Tell me about it!"

Chapter Ten

Mayowa wiped his eyes before holding his son out to have a good look at him. His boy was so gorgeous. He sat on the rug on the floor, and the boy politely sat opposite him.

"Tell me all about you, Femi."

Femi smiled. He could hardly believe Lynx was in his home. What a story to tell his friends!

"My name is Nifemi Cole. I am eight years old…."

He proceeded to tell Lynx about all his favourite things. He talked about his mum being on TV too. And how awesome she was. And his aunt Teju. He loved school. He loved dancing, and he loved singing too. Everyone said he sang very well, he said pointedly.

Lynx smiled, unable to contain his pleasure. Of course, he did.

"I love video games, but I am only allowed to play on my PS 4 on weekends."

"Sounds sensible to me, Femi."

Femi lifted his chin and peering at him through his deep-set eyes, took Lynx by surprise with his next statement.

"Are you friends with my mum?"

Lynx nodded. "Yes, I am. She interviewed me recently."

"I know. I watched. But my mum doesn't have friends. Aunt Teju does."

Lynx was unsure what to say to the boy. Sade did not really let people in, and it could very well be said that he had forced his way into her life nine years earlier.

"Your mum is a special woman."

Femi considered this. "Do you like my mum?"

"I like your mum very much." Lynx smiled.

"So, are you like going to be my daddy? That will be so dope! My real dad is in heaven, you know."

Lynx nearly choked.

Thankfully, just then, Sade walked back in. She had been listening in.

"No, Femi. Your dad is not in heaven." She said calmly and came to sit with both.

Femi looked at her in some confusion.

"Your dad is alive."

"He is alive?"

Sade nodded.

"Where is he, mum?"

She took hold of his hands.

"Right here. Lynx is your father."

Sade panicked as she watched Femi instantly going pale with shock. She looked in concern at Lynx, but his attention was solely on their son.

"Femi," he called softly.

"Are you saying Lynx is my real dad, mum?"

"Yes, son," Lynx said very gently. "I am your dad."

"You didn't die and go to heaven?"

"No, I didn't. Hopefully not for a long time."

"And you never came to see me? You didn't care about me?"

At that moment, Lynx realised he had suddenly stopped being a megastar to their son and become the father who had abandoned him. He could not defend himself without putting Sade in it.

Sade and Lynx spoke at the same time.

"I am sorry…."

"That is my fault…."

"It is my fault," Sade repeated firmly. "Your father didn't know you…you existed… until today. And of course, he wanted to see you immediately."

Femi faced his mother squarely. "You never told him about me? You interviewed him. Why didn't you tell him, mama?"

Femi rarely called her mama unless he was distraught. "You said he went to heaven, mama!"

"I am sorry, Femi."

But Femi was not having it. "You lied to me, mama."

He leapt off the floor and flounced out of the room.

Sade turned to Lynx in distress. "I have never seen him like this."

"He's never dealt with something like this before," Lynx told her, his face strained. He was already off the floor. "I will go to him."

Dejectedly, Sade remained seated on the floor and felt Teju touching her shoulder.

She turned to her and wept. Entropy was the theme of her existence in recent times. Her emotions were chaotic and all over the place. Teju sat with her and reassured her that all would be fine in the end.

"There will always be a calm after the storm. This too will pass."

About half an hour later, Lynx briefly returned to the two women. "He would like to have his dinner in his room." He announced.

Teju put a restraining hand on Sade. "Let me."

Left to her devices, Sade slipped back into the events of the last nine years. She rarely did, but there was nowhere else to go.

Sade grew up in Ebute Metta, a part of the Lagos mainland, home to a central transport terminal. In the end, their bungalow, and a small sum of money, were all their parents had left behind for her and Temilade. Temilade finished high school a few months short of seventeen and had no means of going to university, as their mother had just died. Temilade prioritised looking after her little sister, hoping one day she might get help and be able to return to school. Sade went to school every morning, and Temilade went to work. Sade did not know what she did.

When Temilade tragically died at seventeen, Sade was thirteen. She chose not to live at the mercy of the state or strangers. Besides, who knew who killed her sister?

Queens Grammar was only six kilometres from Ebute Metta and was the closest boarding school. Sade considered it her last hope and approached Principal Davies armed with a report card and a genuine suicide threat.

When she fled Queens Grammar, she had little savings, mainly from the allowance she had received whilst at Queens. She went to Ebute Metta but intended to return to Queens. Her plans had been total avoidance of future contact with Mayowa. Whatever it took.

The bungalow, however, had been overtaken by squatters, who were the unruliest strangers Sade ever saw. Teju was walking by when she stumbled onto Sade as she stood lost in the streets. She recognised Sade instantly. Sade, in turn, remembered Teju as her mother's only friend in the neighbourhood.

Teju and her mother had bonded over the philandering men they married. The difference, though, was that Mrs Cole defended her marriage, and Teju saw hers as what it was. A massive mistake. Teju left her husband and moved out of the neighbourhood a few months before Sade lost her father. However, she had returned upon her husband's sudden passing from a fatal stroke the year before. And to the news of the Cole family tragedy. But no one knew exactly what had become of Sade. Sade had been gone for three years when Teju returned to Ebute Metta, and the police were not interested in helping her look.

So, it was a shock to find Sade randomly standing one day in the hot Lagos sun in front of her old home. Teju took her home and asked where she had been, to which Sade simply responded. "Boarding school."

Those people had been in her home for years, Teju told her. But they would find a legal way to evict them and reclaim the bungalow for Sade. In the meantime, Sade could stay with her for the holidays. Sade told Teju she only had a term left.

"What about university entrance exams?"

"I am writing like everyone else, but I don't know how I can go."

"Don't worry about it. We will get your home back. Rent it out to make money and live here with me."

The vomiting started a few weeks later, just as she was preparing to return to Queens. She was hardly ever sick. Even before the doctor pronounced her pregnant, Sade knew it.

"Who is the father?" Teju asked.

"My life is finished," had been Sade's response.

Teju's attempt at finding out Femi's paternity had been met with a brick wall which led her to conclude that the circumstances of Femi's conception were perhaps traumatic. And that it was probably causing more harm than good to keep pursuing the subject. Teju had been supportive instead. She looked after the pregnant teen as she would her own. Sade got her home back and let out the bungalow as Teju had advised. She lived with Teju and wrote all her outstanding university entrance exams as an external candidate.

Sade secured her job at the newspaper house during the compulsory youth service corps year. The job was on Lagos Island, and the commute was herculean.

She also had misgivings about raising her child in the neighbourhood she grew up in, which held many bad memories.

Teju agreed the neighbourhood was becoming more unsafe as well and not what it had been years earlier.

Both women sold their homes and used the proceeds to buy the Lekki peninsula duplex. It was one of twin duplexes. Her neighbour, the doctor, owned the other. They had been happier here. Happier than they had ever been.

Sade was caught up in her reverie and did not hear Lynx come back to her.

"He's just finished his dinner." He announced. He had brought Femi's plates back down to the kitchen and came to find Sade still sitting on the floor, her back now rested against the sofa.

"How's he?" She asked.

"He will get over it. He loves you."

So, still mad at her.

"He wants me to put him to bed," Lynx said slowly.

"Will you be okay?"

Sade nodded.

He caressed her cheek. "Don't be hard on yourself. You were only a child. I am in awe of the marvel you have achieved, giving what life handed you at a tender age. I should apologise for my teenage hormones and getting you pregnant, yet I can't…."

Sade shook her head, sniffling. "It takes two to tango, Lynx. I was very much a willing participant. Besides, you cannot apologise for that, for which I have absolutely no regrets. I do not regret our son."

"You must know I am thankful. That you kept him."

"Not keeping him was never an option."

Teju walked in from the kitchen just then and asked what they both wanted for dinner.

"I am not hungry." She said as Lynx went to put their son to bed.

"I asked Declan to come back in the morning," he said on his return. "Hope it is okay if I stay the night?"

She put her head against his chest. Rarely did she admit to needing someone, but right then, she needed him.

They later slept in each other's arms, and when Mayowa woke up the next day, she was still there, sound asleep.

He smiled. History was resetting itself. The universe owed him that much. He carefully extricated himself and brushed his teeth in her en suite bathroom with a spare toothbrush. He went down to the kitchen to make himself a cup of coffee.

Teju already had a kettle on the boil.

"Good morning."

"Good morning, Lynx." Teju smiled. "Mayowa, isn't it? I googled you last night."

He laughed, taking a seat at the kitchen island. "Sade renamed me Lynx, you know. But you can always ask me what you want to know. You can't believe everything on the internet."

"I know. It is still all very surreal."

He nodded his agreement. "Up to less than twenty-four hours ago, I had no idea I had a son."

Teju poured the hot water into two mugs. "Tea, chocolate, or coffee?"

"Coffee please, black, no sugar."

"Sade said you were quite furious."

"I was initially, but even as I was, I thought of how hard her life had already been, even before an unwanted pregnancy at seventeen. How can anyone stay mad at her?"

"True, Sade has had a difficult life, but with a lot of determination and luck, she managed to put her life together."

"She tells me you have a lot to do with that."

Teju handed him his drink. She made tea for herself. She sat down opposite him and took a sip.

"Sade is the child I never had, Lynx. The daughter of my friend."

Lynx put down his drink. "You were friends with her mum?"

"Yes, Aisha and I were friends."

Aisha. Lovely name, Lynx thought of the woman who had birthed Sade.

Teju added, "but I wasn't around when she passed, not when her father passed nor when…."

She struggled to finish the sentence.

"When Temilade died." Lynx finished gently, knowing it was a kinder word than murdered.

"Yes, Temilade too."

And Leila.

Teju shook her head as if to clear it. "Sade always said to look into the future and leave the past where it belonged."

Except without dealing with the past, you were not moving on.

"I thank you," Lynx said, keeping his misgivings to himself. "I will eternally be grateful to you for looking after them. For looking after Femi when Sade went back to school."

Teju smiled. "They both gave a purpose to my life."

Sade wandered down just then in a satin house robe. It was the first time he saw her in the early morning, fresh-faced. He swallowed hard. She was so beautiful….

She came to sit next to him. "Talking about me?"

"Yep," Teju replied, smiling secretly to herself. She had just seen the look on Lynx's face as Sade came into the room. He was clearly smitten. She handed Sade a cup of hot chocolate, made her excuses, and left the two alone.

"I didn't hear you get up," Sade said to him.

"I didn't want to wake you. Besides, waking up and finding you still there was quite the novelty."

Sade rolled her eyes. "Are you ever going to let that go?"

"Not for as long as I live." He said, laughing.

Femi flew down the stairs next, shouting Lynx's name. He had woken up and feared last night had only been a dream.

He went to hug his father tightly and said a polite good morning to his mother.

"Would you like to play PS4 with me, Lynx?"

"After your breakfast," Sade said. "Have you brushed your teeth?"

"I will do." He replied shortly.

"And your homework?"

Femi lifted his chin. "Lynx will help me with it."

"Sure," Sade said and got up to make their breakfast. Lynx joined her to prepare a quick breakfast of toast and scrambled eggs.

"Give him a little more time." He whispered to her at the sink.

She brightly put the meal in front of Femi.

Femi chatted about the party he attended the day before, mainly to Lynx. Dele was his best friend, he announced, and his house was pretty cool.

"Is your house pretty cool too?"

"My parents…your grandparents live not too far from here. They have their own beach, and their house is amazing."

Femi turned excitedly in his seat. "I have grandparents?"

"And an aunt too. She lives in New York. They are looking forwards to meeting you soon."

"And cousins?"

Lynx laughed. "No first cousins yet. You are the only Fernandez grandchild."

All their lives were never going to be the same again, Sade thought. Lynx's parents and his sister were on their way to Lagos. She had no idea how they would react and if she had to profusely apologise to them too.

What did Lynx expect of her? She looked over at him. He caught her glance and winked at her. Her heart flipped.

Damn him.

Whenever she thought serious, he easily overtook her thoughts with sexy.

He helped Femi with homework after breakfast, and Sade tidied up back in the kitchen. The duo played football on Femi's PS4, making Sade feel somewhat redundant. She announced she was going upstairs to make herself a bath. Lynx acknowledged this with a tilt of his head while Femi ignored her.

Declan soon arrived with new clothing for his boss, and Lynx introduced Declan to his son.

Declan took the little hand in his massive one. "Very pleased to meet you, Femi."

"Are you like a giant?" Femi asked, open-mouthed at the massive frame. Declan was easily a seven-footer.

"Are you like a Jack?" Declan replied playfully, and Femi laughed.

"I haven't got a bean, Declan."

"You do have this," Lynx pointed at the screen and

handed the wireless controller to Declan. "Keep an eye on him for me, will you?"

"Of course, boss. Teach him a thing or two about soccer too."

Femi chortled. "It's football. Teach me? Bring it on, old man."

Lynx picked up the little bag Declan had brought him and headed for Sade's room. He stripped himself naked in her bedroom and found her submersed in foam in the large oval bath, eyes closed. He smelt lavender and a hint of chamomile. She opened her eyes as he came in. He locked the door behind him. She could not take her eyes off him, off his magnificent body.

"Femi…" She began throatily.

"With Declan," Lynx replied softly, his eyes intent on hers. He stepped into the warm bath behind her, setting her snugly against him. He poured the foamy water over her shoulders, her arms, and her breasts and caressed her nipples gently. Her mouth turned sideways to meet his in a kiss filled with so much desire that he found himself barely hanging on to sanity. He could never have enough of this woman. She felt his hardness against her and brushed her buttocks against him. He slid a hand down and dipped his fingers between her legs, stroking her, feeling the warm wetness inside her and around them. She moaned into his mouth over and over again. He lifted her and set her astride him, pushing deeply inside her. He had a fleeting thought to discuss contraception with her later. She moved against him, pushing down to meet his upward thrusts.

They both climaxed hard. Afterwards, he gently soaped her limp body.

"Back to work tomorrow?" he asked as he lathered her legs.

"Yes, I will be.".

"Tito and my parents are arriving tomorrow morning." He told her.

"What's your sister up to?"

"Nothing except meet her nephew and hopefully bury the hatchet with you?" There was a near plea in his voice. "Tito is a different person these days."

"Funny, I don't remember what exactly started the

fight.”

“I know,” he whispered in her ear. “It’s an alpha female thing.”

Sade giggled.

“Anyway, I hope we can all have a peaceful dinner at my parents’ tomorrow evening?”

“What are your parents like?”

“They are lovely people, even if I say so myself.”

“Where did Tito fall off then?”

Lynx laughed.

“My dad swore she’s off some mafia ancestor.”

Sade laughed again. “Dinner with a mafia.”

“You have your own Smith and Wesson, I have no doubt, and perfectly able to defend yourself, but I assure you, there will be no need.”

Sade relaxed into him.

“Okay, Lynx. If that’s what you want.”

“I very much want, my love.

Chapter Eleven

ynx came the following morning to drop Femi off at school, much to the latter's delight. Teju went with them, and Sade went to work.

On the drive to school, Lynx asked Femi to promise not to tell his friends yet who he was.

"Why not?"

"Because it is not yet time."

"And why not?" Femi persisted.

"I think you should meet your grandparents and aunt first, right?"

By the frustrating expression on his face, Lynx could tell Femi did not see the association between the two actions. Neither did Lynx, but he could not exactly share his fears with the little boy.

"I will announce you to the world, Femi. When you are ready."

"I was born ready."

Teju laughed beside him.

"Okay, what about when we are all ready?"

Lynx stayed back in the car whilst Declan and Teju took Femi in. He wanted to be a normal father who could park and walk his little boy from the car to his classroom. At the same time, he was keen to protect his child from his fame. What if someone found out he had a child in this school and kidnapped him for ransom? There was a spate of kidnappings in the country at present.

He looked at the security around the school. It appeared promising, but that did not stop him from worrying anyway.

Sade told him many local celebrities sent their kids there, and the security was tight. Lynx wanted more.

*****

Sade ruthlessly dived into her work headlong. The weekend had been filled with anger, passion, more anger, and more passion. And it could do a woman's head in if she dwelled on it too much. Femi had thawed somewhat towards her the evening before.

Refusing to let her thoughts linger on the upcoming dinner, she prepared materials and emailed Tony the whole lot.

"Working while on holiday!" He texted with an exploding brain emoji.

She left work thirty minutes earlier than usual to beat the traffic.

Lynx's Landcruiser was parked outside the duplex with his chauffeur and bodyguard in tow. Teju told her Declan had also helped on the afternoon school run. Sade frowned slightly as a thought occurred to her.

She hurriedly changed into a red tailored waterfall dress with cut-out shoulders, V-neck bodice and flowing ruffles. And carefully touched up her makeup.

Femi looked smart and adorable in the mock neck navy blue shirt and brown chino trousers she had put out for him the evening before.

"How do I look, mum?" He asked a little anxiously.

"You look awesome." She lightly brushed a speck off his shirt and kissed his forehead.

"There is something we should probably discuss, not that it matters."

"What, mum?"

"Your grandma. She is…she is white."

Femi looked puzzled by the statement. "Yeah, everyone knows Lynx is mixed race, and he is my dad, so…."

"Well, I didn't want you to be shocked."

"Okay, mum," he half rolled his eyes, "can we go now, please?"

They said their goodbyes to Teju just before her phone rang. It was Lynx asking what time they would be arriving.

"We are just about to leave. Your parents?"

"They arrived this morning. And so did Tito. They are all looking forwards to tonight. How's my boy?"

"He's good. Your staff is still here, Lynx."

"I told them to stay and drive you both over." He explained.

Sade stepped out of the living room with Femi in tow and considered the sight of the chauffeur and bodyguard in front of her.

"I wish you had discussed it with me first."

"I am sorry. I thought I could save you the hassle of driving through the traffic."

"And Declan? The bodyguard?"

Lynx paused for a few seconds. "Okay, you got me. Can we talk about it later, please?"

It would have to be later, as Declan, just then, stepped out of the front seat to open the door for them.

"Of course, see you soon." She told him.

*****

"They are on their way." Lynx went into the large living area and announced to his parents and sister.

"Good." Anna Fernandez clapped her hands together. "Can't wait to meet them both."

Lynx had been regaling his family with stories about his son and Sade. And had shown them pictures and videos on his phone.

"He looks so much like you, Mayowa," Tito said, looking over his shoulder.

"Indeed." Their father, Kunle Fernandez, appeared enthralled by the videos and, turning to his wife, said, "remember darling, when Mayowa was that age?"

Ana retrieved an old family album. The resemblance was uncanny.

Tito flopped next to her mother. "I was thinking we might need DNA," and hastily added at the thunderous expression on her brother's face, "just to be sure but seeing all these photos of your boy, oh boy! Seeing him for the first time on a wall, looking at a mini-Lynx, gosh, what a shock it must have been!"

"It was. I called you, remember?"

"Yeah, and threatened her with me. Can you believe that, mum?"

Anna ignored Tito. "How is she now?"

Lynx smiled happily. "She is fine. We are pretty good. Great together."

"You are together, you and Sade?" Anna asked, a slight wobble in her voice. "Because of your son?"

"No, mum," Tito interjected. "He ditched Michelle the moment he saw Sade again, came back to Lagos to convince her to date him, and accidentally stumbled on his son. Well, his picture anyway. We don't know if otherwise, he would ever have known of his child."

"Really, Tito? That is what you get out of all this?" Lynx was furious. What was it about Sade that brought the animal out of Tito?

Tito had the grace to show some remorse. "Sorry big bro. I was trying to clarify the timeline of events to mum and got carried away."

"It is not your timeline to clarify, is it?" Anna said a little harshly to her daughter. "You and Sade, is tonight going to be a problem?"

"No. I will be the best aunt ever; just you all wait and see."

"And to Sade?" Kunle asked pointedly.

"Sade and I are not teens anymore. Surely there are bigger and happier things in our lives now. I'd very much like to be in my nephew's life, thank you, and I surely can't afford to piss his mum off now, can I?"

They all laughed, and Lynx took his sister to one side.

"Sade is very important to me, Tito."

They went out to take a stroll along the beach.

"I know, Mayowa. I was there in the beginning, wasn't I?"

"So, you of all people should understand."

"I do and yet don't understand it, you know, this true love thing."

"I have been told," Lynx replied mockingly, "that you could go through life and not experience it once." He shook his head. "How terrible!"

Tito laughed. "You are horrible! I will find mine one day."

"It was love at first sight for me," Lynx said on a serious note. "I remember the first time I saw her. She was bending over her friend, Anne. She was and still is the most beautiful human I have ever seen. I have dated over the years, but no one holds a candle to Sade. She is the dream I had when I was younger."

A little tear fell onto Tito's cheeks. "I hope it all goes well this time, Mayowa. I don't wanna see you broken again."

"Don't worry, little sis. This time will be different."

"Is there anything I can do?"

"There are a few, but I doubt you have the time."

"I can make time for family. I can work remotely and fly to New York as often as I must until things are a bit steadier. I can imagine they are not exactly, no?"

Lynx told her about Sade's early losses, how she

came to be at Queens, the pregnancy, and Teju being an informal kind of adopted aunt.

"I cannot even imagine the horror!" Tito exclaimed.

"She was only five years older than Femi is when she came to Queens Grammar, as a last resort, a child with no family. So obviously the question is, where were grandparents, aunties, uncles, cousins, you know, the usual extended family?"

"You think she's not telling you everything? Sade can be…." Tito searched for the right word, "something of an enigma. You have to talk to her."

"There is someone else I should be talking to, but I worry that Sade might think I am digging behind her back, but you are a lawyer and finding out things, well, it is as per your skill set."

"Aunt Teju?" Tito sussed. "I can, but it all boils down to the same thing, doesn't it? Digging behind her back and finding out what she is not ready to share may backfire. Things have a way of coming out with time. A little patience will go a long way. Lynx, I think Sade needed that therapy more than we ever did."

Lynx could not agree more.

*****

Sade had been to the Fernandez home before, but it was a rushed entry. She had left highly strung, shaken to the core by the one-to-one with Lynx, focussing hard on repressing the pains of her past and fighting the physical attractions of the present.

Today, the view was spectacular. Besides her, Femi gasped as they drove from the gated entrance onto the cobblestone driveway, flanked by palm trees whose fronds swayed in the wind. Sade inhaled. She could smell the ocean and the sands, and it brought distant memories of Christmas days spent on the beach. Not this one, obviously, but not too far off.

The Fernandez beach mansion was vast, with stone pillars cladding the façade.

Lynx strode down the small steps between the pillars, looking quite fetching in a navy slim-fitted shirt on stone khaki pants that clung to his alluring physique.

As soon as he safely could, Femi leapt out of the

car into his father's open arms. Lynx lifted him, spun him around, and was amply rewarded with screams of excitement.

Sade walked more leisurely towards the duo, the skirt of her dress undulating in the wind. Lynx put his screaming son down, and she glided effortlessly into his arms.

"You take my breath away. Every single time." He whispered into her ear.

She put her arms around his neck and offered her lips up for a kiss which he gladly obliged.

"You are gorgeous yourself."

He smiled, a happy man. "Come, let us go in."

They walked through a magnificent double door into a glamourous foyer of gold marble flooring. Directly opposite them was a beautiful open-arm staircase with a wrought iron railing. The ceiling was adorned with spiral-shaped crystal chandeliers.

The foyer led into a brightly lit large living area where the Fernandez awaited. And all stood up at the same time as the trio walked in.

It was unclear who gasped first between Tito and

Anna. Anna was Italian-American, a dark-haired, tall, and slim woman, about the same height as her husband, but incredibly strong, Sade found, as she brought both mother and child into a big warm hug. One arm was fiercely around Sade's neck and the other around her grandson's back.

"Well, mum and dad, meet Sade and Femi," Lynx said behind them.

Anna sobbed quietly. Lynx looked over at his dad, who appeared to be wiping a tear or two from his eyes too, and then came quietly into the embrace, followed by Tito. Lynx joined in the emotions of the moment as well.

After what seemed like a long time, Anna finally held Sade at arm's length while Kunle scooped Femi up into his arms.

"You are even more beautiful than reported. More so than on the TV." Anna told Sade breathlessly.

Sade looked surprised.

"Oh, I watch you," Anna confessed. "When you joined ACE, Tito called one day and said Sade Cole is on TV, and I said I must see…glimpse what my boy saw all those years ago. The brains and beauty combined, oh my God. Enough to intimidate mere mortals, my dear."

"Thank you. You are so kind." Sade was mesmerised by Anna's eyes. She saw those eyes every day in her son.

"It's the truth and not mere kindness. Oh, we have so much to talk about…oh, my grandson…so gorgeous…."

Femi's head was on his grandfather's shoulder. Kunle was rubbing his head and had begun the Fernandez family praise poetry in Yoruba, so eloquent and with words so powerful it brought more tears to the eyes.

"Thank you," he finally said to Sade. "You have made this old man very happy. Thank you."

Sade felt a pang of guilt. "I am sorry. I am…"

"No, my dear," Kunle told her. "We are sorry. I apologise on behalf of this one here." He said in Lynx's direction. "And, of course, I am beyond delighted to meet you. As Anna said, we have been watching you on TV, but nothing beats meeting you in person."

"The honour is all mine, sir," Sade said in awe of the love she was being showered.

Kunle was a middle-aged man, quite good-looking with a dignified head of grey hair. His well-defined jaw line was familiar.

"One more person to meet, or shall I say reunite with," Lynx gently extricated Sade from his mother's hold and steered her right into a waiting Tito.

"We meet again," Tito said, her face expressionless.

"Indeed, we do," Sade replied coldly.

Lynx was shocked. Even after all said and done, after all these years…

Both women turned to him and burst into laughter at the priceless expression on his face, going into each other's arms and hugging tightly.

"What?" Lynx asked. "When?"

"Let's just say I have my ways of getting people's phone numbers, shall we?" Tito told him, a wide grin on her face.

"Cutthroat lawyer, remember?" Sade teased him.

"Ahh, okay, you both got me. But when?"

"Tito called this afternoon, just before I left work, and we did a little catch-up."

"And came up with this plan to mess around with my head?"

Tito laughed. "Yep, that one."

And so began a delightful evening indeed. Sade spoke at length with Lynx's parents. They were not kidding when they said they watched her interviews. They were particularly impressed with her take on contemporary issues and her ideology.

They prodded on Femi's birth and his first few years. Sade explained Teju's role in both of their lives and how she had made going back to school possible.

"We must meet this angel," Anna said, another tear rolling down a cheek. "Please, you must introduce us."

"I will do. She will be delighted to meet you too."

Anna showed Sade the old family albums.

"I had them both in Chicago at the Prentice women's hospital. Both beautiful babies, even if I say so myself."

"Is that Lynx and aunt Tito?" Femi said out loud at

a hilarious picture of the siblings, wearing only knickers and their faces covered in a powdery substance.

"Yes, indeed," Kunle replied. "Both their hands literally caught in their mother's make-up jar."

They all laughed as the siblings covered both their faces in a gesture of shame.

"He calls you Lynx?" Tito whispered to her brother.

Lynx smiled. "Yet to earn dad, and yet you get aunt straight away. How unfair!"

"Easy. Do you not know aunts and uncles get all the fun and none of the responsibilities?"

Sade found the Fernandez easy to be around. They teased each other a lot. Tito had grown more pleasant, sophisticated, and poised. And was very good with kids too, Sade found to her surprise. She bonded with Femi over his favourite characters.

"Thor? Yeah, we all love Hemsworth, don't we?" She winked at Sade, who laughed at the scowl on Lynx's face.

"Chris has got nothing on you," Sade told him, still

laughing.

"Shall we go into the dining room and put some food in our bellies?" Anna announced to the group.

They finished the evening with an exquisite spread of rice in different ways, mildly spiced sauces, barbecued fish and chicken, grilled meat, and deliciously cooked lobster in lemon and herb butter sauce. There were chargrilled marinated vegetables for Tito.

When it was time to leave, the elderly couple looked downtrodden.

"Can he spend the night, please, Sade?" Tito asked. "I promise to get him to bed immediately and in school on time tomorrow."

Anna put her two hands together to join in the plea. Kunle hovered around anxiously. How could anyone say no?

"Of course." Sade smiled. "I will send his school wears back with Declan."

Femi yelped his excitement, and Sade felt somewhat betrayed. Which did not make any sense as she knew how much her son loved her. She kissed him goodnight, hugged his grandparents and aunt, and said goodbyes to them too.

Lynx fell in step with her, putting his arms around her shoulders.

"Did you feel pressured back there, my love?"

"Not really," Sade replied, "it was the right thing to do."

"I don't want you to leave." He announced.

"I have to, Lynx."

"Sade, I was thinking of buying my own place in Lagos on my way from LA."

He paused to gauge her reaction, but she said nothing.

"I hadn't given it much thought before, to be honest. I did not need to." He continued. "My parents' home always seemed to suffice in Nigeria, but now, with you and Femi, I feel it is time."

She paused in her stride to look at him under the moon's full light. "You don't want to keep us hidden, and yet you worry about the possible consequences of everyone knowing about us," she said.

"True." He acquiesced.

"So, you want to ensconce us in a high-level security home and have constant armed protection around us? Is this why Declan has been hovering around all day?"

He nodded, a hand framing her face. "I worry you are both sitting ducks if you stay where you are now, and some unscrupulous fellows find out what you are to me. People do anything for money."

"Your world is about to absorb mine, Lynx."

"I see only one world, Sade. A world in which I want to protect the woman I love and our son."

She inhaled shakily. It was not lost on him.

The other hand came to frame the other side of her face.

"I have not been able to say it to anyone else since I said it to you. You ruined me for all women for all time. It has always been you. I love you."

She put her arms around his neck and hugged him tightly.

"It's always, always been you too," she whispered against his cheek. "I loved you then, and I love you still."

"Say it again, Sade. Say it."

"I love you. I love you so much it scares me."

He planted little kisses over her brows, cheeks, down the side of her mouth to her beautiful neck.

"There is absolutely nothing to fear. I'd rather chop off my head than hurt you."

She giggled. "Please don't do that."

"Let's go home."

"Home?"

"Home is wherever you are. Declan and I will return in the morning with Femi's uniform. I dare say I ain't looking forwards to prising myself from your arms in the morning to execute that task."

"Your family…"

"Understand I have years of catching up to do. Come on."

He lifted her off her feet to the car, where Declan waited patiently with an open door. Lynx had, earlier on, sent the chauffeur away. Lynx settled Sade into the car and got in after her.

"Our son will be fine tonight," he told her reassuringly.

She put her head on his shoulder as the car pulled away. The night, him, all of it, felt like magic. Surreal.

Chapter Twelve

Over the next few weeks, they were only apart when Sade was at work. Lynx spent the equivalent time in the studio. She knew he was writing new music. They spent their time together in between the Peninsula and the Fernandez Victoria Island beach home, much to the pleasure of Anna and Kunle, who got to see their grandson more often.

They generally snuck around under the covers of the dark, in the early mornings and late evenings, to avoid unsolicited attention. Lynx hated the sneaking about, but he had also learnt to move at Sade's pace. His parents met Teju, and they all became fast friends.

Tito flew back to New York a week after, but she called regularly. Sade found out Tito was big on gifts. She randomly texted pictures of the things she had bought.

"Hi, Sade, I know you are probably sleeping now, but I was walking along Saks Avenue, and I saw this pair of gorgeous red Louboutin and thought how perfect they would look on you. Anyway, I have couriered them over, and you should have them in the next couple of days. Ciao!"

Then a few days later. "Oh, Sade, I found this lovely Hermes bag today and thought about how well it would go with your red dress, you know, the one you were wearing when you interviewed brother dearest. Anyway, it's on its way to you. Love to my nephew."

And a couple of days later. "Hey, Sade. The new iPhone is coming out next month, and I am thinking of pre-ordering it for Femi; what do you think?"

"Your sister is a shopaholic!" Sade announced to Lynx.

"Aye, that she is. Is she bothering you?"

"I am not sure designer bags and shoes should bother anyone, but your sister is becoming uncontrollable. I don't know how often I can say thanks without feeling like a charity case. And I can't ask her to stop without hurting her feelings."

He nodded unsympathetically. "I can see the dilemma."

"You didn't put her up to this, did you?" She eyed

him suspiciously.

Lynx shook his head. "No, I didn't, but I can guarantee she also buys for herself whatever she is gifting you. Loads of self-love there."

Sade looked unconvinced. It was a Saturday, and they were at the mansion. Teju was having lunch with Anna and Kunle, and Femi was with them. Sade and Lynx were in his quarters.

Sade was curled up in his arms on the sofa, and they were binging on the game of thrones series.

"How much do corporate lawyers in New York earn anyway?" Sade mused out loud, and Lynx burst out laughing.

"A lot. But anyway, there was a Fernandez wealth long before there was a Lynx or Tito wealth. It's old money."

She looked at him with a mocking disapproving smile. "Spoilt brats."

He bent his head and lightly kissed her neck. It tingled as always. "This brat you fell for…."

She giggled. "Yes, this one brat I fell for…sounds like the title of a song."

"Talking of which, there's something I have wanted to discuss with you." He stopped teasing her neck and sounded serious.

"Is all okay?" Sade asked.

"Yeah," he drawled. "I have been working in the studio, as you know."

"Hmm," Sade murmured. "Perfecting a masterpiece?"

"I am not sure it needs perfecting, to be honest. I just need the world to hear it as I have. As you have… heart of this prince."

"Dad's song?"

"Yes, but I need your approval." He continued, "it's such a beautiful song. It's your decision, of course, as it is your legacy. But that song has always called to me. I connected with it on day one. It felt like he understood what it meant to really love someone, like he was deeply in love…."

"He was alright. Just with the wrong her." Sade said intensely.

Lynx knew she was talking about her father and his unfaithfulness.

"It's a beautiful song." She concurred. "We sang it together, him and me, you know. For all his faults, he loved me."

"Of course, he did. How could he not?"

"But a father should love his kids equally, no?"

Lynx listened and said nothing, sensing a shift in their relationship to a place of trust, where she might finally be able to open up to him about her childhood fully.

"No, but he couldn't. And Temilade knew he loved me more, but she didn't resent me for it. Not a bit. Instead, she turned to our mother. And my mother was lovely. She was the best. She showered her love equally."

Lynx massaged her back slowly. What he heard was that Sade had been loved by both parents. It sounded reassuring. He doubted every parent loved their children equally, but the trick surely was in not showing it.

"How did your parents pass?" He already knew Temilade had been murdered, and he did not think he could ever ask that she revisit that tragic memory.

"He died in a car accident. And she died a few months later. She died of heartbreak. Did you even know that was a thing?"

Lynx didn't.

"She just couldn't go on without him. He wasn't even good to her. Why weren't we enough to make her want to live? I mean, she literally willed her own heart to stop."

"And there was no one to look after you two?" Lynx asked carefully. "Aunts, uncles, cousins, grandparents?"

"There was no one," she replied. "My parents grew up in an orphanage. They all did. They were of Fulani-Arabian descent. Their folks were nomads in Yorubaland. They were cattle grazers, Fulani herdsmen. There was a conflict with the farmers. The Fulanis lost out, being in the minorities, you see. Only a few kids were left, and they ended up in an orphanage."

"You are Fulani!" Lynx exclaimed.

She shrugged. "By descent, I suppose, but all my life, all I know of is being Yoruba."

He pushed his fingers into her long soft mane. "Your hair. I have always wondered. But your last name, Cole?"

"Nat King Cole." She replied easily. "My father's all-time favourite. Unforgettable was his most cherished song."

"I am so sorry, love. For all the pain you carry inside. Thanks for sharing that with me. I want more unhindered moments like this with you. In our own place."

"With that again?" Sade asked.

"Why not, my love?"

He kissed her passionately on the lips and muttered into her mouth. "What do you think of Banana Island?"

"Oh, you are shameless. Are you trying to kiss the consent out of me?"

"Is it working?" His hands moved down to cup her buttocks. He gave a little squeeze.

She moaned softly. She was tired of sneaking around as well.

"Sure, it is working. I love Banana Island."

Anna sent a trusted high-end estate company their way. The agent provided them with a detailed brochure. Lynx and Sade argued about the size of the proposed home and eventually, as a compromise, agreed to let Femi have the final say.

Lynx wanted a big family-sized home, and Sade wanted something smaller.

"Whatever my boy wants, he shall get, right?" Lynx said.

"You do know there is something as overindulging a child, don't you?" Sade countered.

"Yes, but on this one, are we agreed he gets his way?"

Femi pointed to the picture of a seven-bedroom mansion whose front view was characterised by four great pillars overlooking a water fountain and supporting a true balcony that could accommodate an intimate evening party.

"Are you sure, Femi?" Sade asked, turning several pages onto the next house.

Femi promptly turned the pages back.

"Look, mum," he pointed at the fountain. "I love this one."

Lynx smiled mischievously. "We love this one, Sade."

Sade was sure Lynx had put their son up to it but had no proof.

"This is your handwork. I can't prove it, but rest assured, I have my eyes on you."

"I should hope so. We wouldn't want you looking at another man now, would we, right son?"

Femi laughed. "No, we would not." He said shortly and continued to stare at the fountain for a while before turning on to the next page.

The mansion housed seven bedrooms, four ensuites, a study, a game room, and three family bathrooms. It had a lovely spiral staircase leading down to its foyer. There was a side garage big enough to accommodate ten cars. There was an excellent view of the Lagos lagoon from the spacious back garden with speed boats in the background.

"Look, mum," Femi squealed as he spotted the

boats on the page. "I want to go in one of those!"

"I am sure, you do," Sade murmured. "Go and play in your room. I want to talk to your daddy."

Femi made his way out of the room, grumbling about never being on a speed boat.

Sade rolled her eyes.

"Look, Sade," Lynx began. "I am not overindulging him, but we do need our own place: an appropriate place, my love. Your neighbour is amazing. It must be from all that confidentiality thing doctors sign up to for life or something, but it's only a matter of time before the press finds out about us. You are both so exposed here, and Femi's school… oh, we need to talk about that and change his school…."

Sade interrupted him. "Lynx, stop. Let's take a deep breath."

"I am breathing just fine. I am just facing our reality head on."

"The reality, Lynx, is that you live in LA." She blurted out.

He paused for a minute. A minute where they stared at each other in silence. Sade broke the silence.

"We need to talk."

"Sounds like we do." He agreed, reaching out to hold one of her hands. "Talk to me."

"These past few weeks have been the best time in my life." Sade told him. "Seeing our boy finally having his father in his life and watching your bond is beyond what I can put into words. You are a great dad. And as a partner," a tear slipped down her cheek, "no one could ask for more. To think of all the years I could have had you if I wasn't so broken…."

"Hey, come here," he brought her into his arms. "Que sera, sera. Now and the future is all that matters."

"That's just it. I don't know how to plan today with you, Lynx. I live here. Our son is here. You live in LA. My job and your music are on different continents. You have an entire management team, security details, your record label, and there is Primetime. Everything is all over the place, and me, you, and Femi are in the middle of everything, and on this board, I don't know where we place us. We are buying a house here. You have one in LA. Are you going to be coming and going? Are we going to be going and coming? You are going to go on tours. Our jobs, Femi's school...."

She threw up her arms in despair. "We can't just buy a multimillion-dollar house without knowing if we are even going to be able to live in it or not."

He kissed the top of her head. "I know exactly what you mean. First of all, I can make my music anywhere. Here, LA, Honolulu, anywhere. Second, do you know what I was doing last year when Tito called me to say she'd found you?"

Sade hid a smile. "You were on tour."

"Were you keeping tabs on me?"

She raised a finger. "First, you are my child's father, so I needed to know what you were up to."

"And?" There was a hint of amusement in his voice.

"Knowing that was a balm on my ego when you told me you had known precisely where I was a year ago. I told myself it was why you couldn't reach out."

"Partly. But much work went into buying ACE and headhunting you, making you secure in my company. You just didn't know it."

"Machiavelli."

"Not really. It was more like a strong belief in your talent, as I saw it back then. So, I was on tour for eighteen months. It was draining, and even as I was finishing it, I knew I couldn't do that anymore. And so, I invested in Primetime and became a businessman in the entertainment industry I am already part of and love."

"You wouldn't tour anymore?"

"I could do it for a month, tops. I have you. We have a terrific son. There is nothing on the road for me that could compare with what I now have. I feel so incredibly blessed."

She trembled slightly in his arms. He moved her. He always moved her.

"There are members of my management team I can coordinate with from any part of the world, but there are those who need to be nearby, like my PA. Security details? We do need them, my love."

"We have to have bodyguards?"

"Please. People are less likely to mess around with you if you have security about you."

"I think I will feel caged."

"You've been around Declan; did you feel caged?"

"No, but that's because I see him as your bodyguard, nothing to do with me."

Lynx laughed. "Declan knew to protect you and Femi from the day he met you. Even now, as we speak, he is doing his job."

Sade knew Declan was always about, but she had chosen to see him as more for Lynx.

"I will think about it."

"That is good enough for me."

"So, you think we can do this?"

"We can. Sade, you, and Femi are my priority."

She put a hand to his face and said, "I have an idea."

"Tell me."

"How about we live here during term time, and stay in LA during the holidays? We can try that for a couple of years and together decide where we are happiest at. I can prerecord interviews throughout the term while you do your music and business at the same time. That way, we get to come home to each other every day."

"I love that." He especially loved that she saw years with him. "We will go on holidays to other places too and see if we fancy other spots on the planet. Just one more thing."

"What?"

"Aunt Teju. She has been a part of both of your lives for a long time. How would she feel about continuing to be? She will have her suite. It is a big house."

"I will have to discuss it with her. She may have other plans, but she does love an extravagant lifestyle." Sade chuckled.

"We could officially pay her as… I don't know…. What does she do for money?" Lynx asked.

"She has a couple of commercial properties and gets rental income. But all she truly cares about is the bond we have built over the years. She never had kids of her own. She has a brother and a sister who live outside Lagos, a few nephews and nieces, and some cousins here and there. Her siblings are nice gentle folks, but they have their own families. Femi and I are hers."

"And now me."

"She will be so thrilled if she hears you say that. You have no idea how trying it is for her to keep us a secret. It's killing her not to be able to brag to her friends!"

Lynx laughed. "And you? Ready to show me to the world."

"Isn't it the other way around?"

"No," he said emphatically. "Left to me, I would move all of us to the beach house this evening and call a press conference tomorrow morning."

"You would move us to your parents'? How matured!"

"Okay, that didn't come out great. Let's close on the house, move in, call that press conference and then leave town. We should all go somewhere for a little holiday. Half-term is just around the corner. I love St Tropez this time of the year."

"St Tropez? The only spot on the planet I have missed. Tell me all about it." Sade replied, her eyes twinkling with mischief. She had only been to Paris and Dubai, and he knew this.

"How about I show you instead?" he said, his eyes and voice packed with innuendo as he lowered his mouth to hers. "Show you some St Tropez," he whispered into her mouth.

She smiled against his lips. "With an awake child in the house?"

"Damn!"

Sade laughed at his frustration.

Chapter Thirteen

vents of the next three weeks mostly happened in a blur. Sade and Teju went to look at five properties the following Saturday. Teju loved the seven-bedroom mansion as Femi had, and Sade had to admit it was regal indeed. Lynx immediately got his accountant and lawyer to make the project their priority.

Teju made a list of the top interior decorator companies, and it was eerie to see how similar it was to Anna's. Sade had the final say with many nudges from the two women. Finally, she gave up pretending she knew anything about the minefield interior decoration was, and happily allowed the two women to take the reign, which freed her to concentrate on prerecording a few interviews before the planned St. Tropez getaway. They consulted her on major decisions on general themes, colours, furniture, and draperies but happily met each other regularly "on-site" to discuss the progress of their work. Sade had never seen Teju more in her elements.

"Mum can't stop talking about aunt Teju," Lynx told Sade one evening. "They seem to do everything together these days. I was on-site with them today, and my own mother ignored me most of the time."

"And gone completely over the top with it as well!" Sade exclaimed. "I have told them to slow down. We can finish the decorations when we return from France."

Two days before St Tropez, they moved into their new grand home. Sade and Teju had decided to rent out their Lekki Peninsula duplex.

A day before St Tropez, Lynx and Sade called a press conference and went public with their relationship. The reporters went into a frenzy at the news of the couple's eight-year-old son.

"So, you didn't just meet then…."

"No. Sade and I met nearly a decade ago but went our separate ways soon after."

"You must have been teenagers…."

"Yep, we were," Sade replied. "I was seventeen, and he was nineteen. I interviewed him for the school Term magazine at the time."

"And you got pregnant?"

A bit silly that, but Sade obliged the question.

"I did…and I moved away…from Lynx at the time."

"What does that mean, Sade?"

"We broke up," Sade told the eager young reporter from the Punch. Besides her, Lynx squeezed her hand.

"So, you kept your child a secret from…?"

"We kept our child protected," Lynx interjected.

"What's his name?"

"Nifemi," Lynx replied.

"Lynx, nine years ago, was about the same time you had your career break, came back three years later with a name change and a transition to afrobeats. Was it to do with Sade, your child's birth and your breakup?"

Lynx and Sade looked at each other, and all cameras zoomed in on the look.

"Sade renamed me Lynx." He admitted and paused at the general widespread murmur in the room and continued as it slowly ebbed. "She thought at the time I should be an afrobeats artiste; she felt I could do wonders with the genre, and it could do wonders with me too."

"Sade was a smart teenager…" a reporter interrupted from the back of the room, and everyone laughed.

Lynx continued after the laughter had died down. "So, when we parted ways at the time, it was hard… hard for both of us, and I went to America and left the music scene for a while to finish school."

"Aww, a heartbreak?"

Lynx grinned. "You could say that."

"Did you abandon your child Lynx?"

"No, he didn't," Sade said calmly. "He is an amazing father."

"At your recent interview of Lynx, Sade, you asked him about the inspiration from his past who influenced his transition to afrobeats; weren't you in effect asking about yourself?"

"He wouldn't shut up about it," Sade teased Lynx. "I am a very private person, and Lynx knew I wouldn't want to be outed, but for the sake of the interview, we had to discuss his musical influences, if that makes sense?"

"It does." The reporter muttered.

"It is well known that Lynx didn't do TV interviews. But was that what brought you two together again?"

Lynx leaned slightly into the microphone. "In a way, yes, but the heart of this Lynx has always belonged to this girl…."

That was the headliner for nearly all the major news outlets the following morning.

*****

They switched off their phones and flew to France the next day in Lynx's private jet with a super excited Femi and Teju.

"Now, my friends will believe me," Femi announced on the flight.

They were watching the press conference on the large screen TV. Femi sat in between his parents on a three-seater leather sofa. Teju was sitting adjacent on a recliner sofa. The décor of the private jet was in shades and tones of dark brown and beige.

"You have been telling your friends?" Lynx asked incredulously. "You promised."

Femi had the grace to put up a crestfallen face. "Sorry."

Sade giggled. "You believed an eight-year-old was going to keep that massive secret?"

"I could hardly keep it in myself," Teju added.

"So, you knew he would tell all his friends?"

The two women nodded in unison. "Oh, absolutely," Sade said.

"And?"

"Kids tell tales all the time, and they have pretend friends. They don't always believe each other, especially when the tale seems quite far-fetched. Even though he looks like you, there is still a massive disbelief factor. Like wow!"

"Okay, my bad." Lynx rubbed his son's head. "Sorry, kiddo, that was too much of an ask."

Femi hugged his father. "I promise not to break another promise."

Lynx laughed, wrapping his arms around the little boy. "And I promise not to make you promise the impossible!"

*****

They landed at La Mole six hours later, where a chauffeured seven-seater Benz jeep met them. There was another minivan, which Lynx explained would follow on with their luggage. Femi slept on the short journey and only woke up when they arrived at Les Parcs De St Tropez.

They were met outside by the concierge, a man in his mid-thirties.

"Bienvenue Monsieur Fernandez, mademoiselle et madame," he greeted them. "Je m'appelle Philippe. Avez-vous fait bon voyage?"

"Oui tout s'est bien passé, merci." Lynx answered effortlessly. Besides him, Femi giggled.

"My dad speaks French!"

"And Italian," Sade told him. When she first interviewed him years ago, Lynx had told her he spoke three languages- Yoruba, English, and Italian. He added French later during his career break.

"Excusez-moi. On m'a dit que tu parlais francais."

Philippe said a bit flustered and switched to English. "I do speak English."

"C'est le cas," Lynx replied in a reassuring voice and switched as well. "But my girlfriend and son don't."

Philippe took them on a tour of the villa. It was on an exquisitely landscaped plot with a stunning sea view. Outdoors was a pool house and a heated infinity pool bothered by sun loungers. A large living room on the ground floor opened onto a furnished terrace facing the sea and the swimming pool. There was a large kitchen with a central island and a cold room with direct access through a service entrance. Two staff bedrooms had their own service entrance, bathrooms, and kitchen. Close by was a laundry room.

The first floor hosted two master bedrooms with king-sized beds, walk-in closets, bathrooms, and sea views. Three other smaller rooms overlooked the landscaped gardens and had a partial ocean view. There was an office from where they caught a glimpse of the pier, beyond which they saw some boats and yachts in the distance. Lynx promised his son they would go on a boat the next day, to which Femi expressed his delight with a tight hug and a little jig.

The villa came with a dedicated staff of a chef and housekeeper, whom Philippe introduced as Raphael and Natalie.

Sade was enthralled at the sheer beauty of the villa and its spectacular décor. Teju was wide-eyed as she looked around as well.

"I must have done something right in a past life." She said to Sade in Yoruba, who laughed and turned to Lynx.

"This place is so beautiful, Mayowa."

"I am glad you like it."

The minivan soon arrived, and Philippe brought in their luggage and helped Natalie put them away in the rooms.

"Where is Declan?" Sade looked around.

"Scrutinising the video surveillance and perimeter alarm," Lynx replied.

Sade put her arms around him. "And so begins our vacation."

He kissed her forehead. "Here, I will not be

competing with ACE for your attention. I am beginning to resent my own company. Come, let's go to our rooms."

Natalie had put their luggage in the bigger Master bedroom and Teju's in the smaller one. Femi's room was closer to his parents, and Declan's faced his.

Dinner was a delicious meal of lobster bisque, chicken in wine sauce, beef bourguignon, seasoned melted goat cheese, and crème brulee. There was a basket of baguettes in the centre of the dinner table.

"The French love their bread, don't they?" Sade recollected fondly.

Lynx laughed. "I don't particularly like baguettes. Too hard for my palate."

"And your son's too, apparently," Sade told him. "He prefers brioche. I am partial to some croissants myself."

Lynx nodded. "I love brioche. Soft and buttery. What's there not to like?"

Teju declared herself extremely tired after the meal and bid them all goodnight. Sade put Femi to bed as well, with a broad smile on his face.

"We are going on a boat tomorrow, mum."

"Not if you don't go to sleep on time."

Femi promptly shut his eyes tight. "Good night, mum."

Sade smiled, kissed his forehead, and put out the light.

*****

It was late morning, being mildly jet lagged from the previous day's travel, that they made their way to the pier, where a navy blue and white mid-sized boat awaited them.

Teju excused herself from the day trip, pleading predisposition to sea sickness. It was a lovely sunny day and a day to be out and about.

Sade was pleasantly surprised, and Femi screamed when he saw the boat was named Nifemi.

"Thank you, dad!" He jumped up and down excitedly, and Sade held on to him out of fear he may jump off the pier.

It was also the first time Femi directly addressed Lynx as dad; the moment was not lost on either of them. Sade and Lynx smiled at each other, silently acknowledging the milestone.

"You've made him very happy. I don't know what it is about him and boats." She said, remembering their boat trip on the river Seine which Femi had tearfully insisted on but had not been part of their original plans.

"I bought it a couple of years ago," Lynx told Sade. "And had it named Nifemi once I found out he was into boats. It was docked last night."

Sade was a bit worried about being out on the sea. Lynx assured her they had everything they needed as he helped Femi and then Sade on board.

"Including all rescue gear…." He teased mercilessly.

Raphael joined them on the boat and informed Sade that Natalie would prepare lunch for Teju and make a start on dinner later in the day.

"Declan is our sailor today."

"A man of many talents," Sade observed.

"A useful skill if you need to make a quick getaway." Declan grinned.

In a life jacket, Femi quickly declared his

intentions to assume a seat next to Declan at the helm.

"We will set sail soon, young man," Declan told him fondly.

In the cabin, Sade switched her phone back on. Lynx was surprised she had brought it on board and reminded her they had decided on a digital detox holiday. Teju and Declan had their phones on if there was a family emergency.

"I can't be in the middle of the Mediterranean without being able to…."

"Call for help? We will barely be on the edge of the Mediterranean."

"I know. What if aunt Teju needs us?"

"She has Declan's number. And emergency numbers. And Natalie."

"And if we need help?"

"We will transmit May Day."

"Okay, okay. You win." Sade was about to switch the phone off when an opportune ring came through.

"Told you," Lynx said.

"It's your sister."

He put his two palms together in a plea. "Please,

please do let it ring out. I love my sister. I swear I do, but can we just enjoy this time together uninterrupted?"

Sade obliged him.

"There are ten missed calls from her. She's probably been trying to get hold of you too. Maybe we should call her back?"

"More likely than not, it is about the press conference," Lynx assured her. Sade switched off her phone a tad reluctantly.

"We don't want to be banging on about that, do we?" He lazily pulled her into his arms. "And why is my sister trying to ruin our holiday?"

His voice was low and seductive. He kissed her lips, initially ever so lightly. Then his tongue easily slid into her open mouth. If his plan was to switch her thoughts away from his sister and onto him, it was a great success.

Her arms went around his neck and pulled the back of his head even closer. As his mouth pleasured hers, his hands went to her back, slowly unzipped her flowery cotton dress and unhooked her bra, baring her full breasts to him.

"I love your body. I love every part of you." He whispered, his mouth travelling down her neck and coming to rest on a nipple which he took into his mouth. Sade moaned, feeling her legs going weak under her. He lifted her off her feet and onto the bed. She felt the soft sheets on her back and Lynx's hard body on hers. She pulled his t-shirt over his head, and he assisted by lifting his mouth off her breast for a few seconds. He had one hand rubbing her other breast in a circular motion while the other hand travelled down her flat belly, finding its way into her pants, which he dismissed speedily.

She was completely naked, and he loved every inch of her. He stood momentarily to take off his trousers and put on protection, his eyes unwaveringly intent on her.

He was gorgeous, this man of hers, Sade thought in immense pleasure of his male form and holding his gaze steady. She loved him more than she thought she could ever love a man. It sometimes scared her, but she felt more secure in her powers over him.

He fitted her snugly, and Sade wrapped her legs around his waist and felt his restraint as he paced his thrust slowly, his mouth back on hers, his hands supporting her hips. She grazed his back lightly, and her hands came to rest on his sexy backside, pulling him deeper into her. He steadily picked up the pace to match her needs, whispering loving words into her ears.

"I love you." She told him, her voice raw with that emotion.

"And I love you." He responded. "I will always love you."

He moved his hands to her backside, lifting her to meet his plunges, which had picked up a faster pace. She met him thrust for thrust, clenching her muscles tight around him. He moaned into her mouth; his tongue entwined around hers.

The explosion of sensation in her core was accompanied by the quickening of his breath, his pelvis slamming deeply into hers such that their bodies became one. He tightened his grip on her buttocks while his shuddering thrusts hit the centre of her being.

"You are killing me slowly, woman," Lynx said moments later, rolling onto his back and feeling every muscle in his body at peace from their lovemaking.

She traced his jawline with a finger, smiling smugly. "I do remember a certain youngster with enormous confidence in his powers to charm women."

He laughed. "In fairness, you'd ensnared me first, and I was hoping to return the favour."

She smiled lazily at him, licking the bottom of her lips, her fingers slowly and provocatively travelling down her flat belly to her mound. "Oh, how you've returned the favour, Mayowa Fernandez."

Unable to resist the temptation, Lynx turned her over and kissed her lovely behind, slowly moving up her back and shoulders. His arms went around her lower belly, lifting her to receive him again. Sade screamed her pleasure into the pillow as he thrust in and out of her until they both reached climax together, and he fell onto her back.

*****

They went up to the lounge on the deck half an

hour later to enjoy the view of the Mediterranean. Raphael brought drinks in a bucket of ice. Femi was apparently learning the art of sailing and was glued to Declan's side and only joined them for lunch.

They were at Sainte Maxime. Raphael acted as their tour guide. He told them the beach was at the centre of the liberation of Southern France from the Germans during the second world war. It was a sister city to Bellport in New York. St Tropez was the first town on its coast to be liberated as part of operation dragoon.

The views of the Massif de l'Esterel mountains as they plunged into the Mediterranean Sea were truly impressive. The red colour of the hills, Sade leant, resulted from their volcanic origin. The Riviera took them to Cannes.

Sade mainly relaxed and enjoyed the views of the hills and mountains, the fishing villages, and the historical backdrop from Raphael.

Raphael described Antibes as originally being found as a Greek colony. It was initially named Antipolis from its position on the opposite side of the river estuary from Nice. In 1815, Napoleon had escaped exile on the island of Elba in Tuscany and had hoped for a warm welcome in Antibes, as they had been supportive of his reign, but the people closed their gates to him, and he was left with no choice but to move on northward without stopping.

"Some friends," Sade commented, and Raphael laughed.

In Nice, they saw tourists, cyclists, families, and skateboarders along the Promenade des Anglais.

They headed back to St Tropez, where they expected to arrive later in the afternoon.

"We should explore St Tropez tomorrow." Sade stretched. "It is, after all, the place to be."

Lynx crinkled his nostrils. "Declan told me some of my acquittances are in town," he confessed. "I hope to have us all to ourselves for a couple of days before you meet the crowd."

"Of course." She planted a kiss on his lips. They wanted the same things. He helped her off the boat when they returned to the Les Parcs pier and kept hold of her hand. Close behind were Femi, Raphael, and

Declan.

They found Teju lounging by the poolside, a magazine in hand, and crawling down the pool, jet lag be damned, was the slender figure of Tito Fernandez.

"Hi, bro!" She called out, laughing at the frank disbelief on her brother's face.

Chapter Fourteen

"**A**unt Tito!"

Femi ran excitedly from behind his parents to his equally happy aunt at the poolside.

"I can drive a boat! Declan taught me!"

"Really?" Tito gracefully climbed out of the pool and lifted her nephew.

"Phew, you've grown bigger than last I saw you!"

Femi wriggled. "Aunt Tito, you are making my clothes wet!"

"Who cares? We will have you changed in a minute. I have missed you."

She was wearing a turquoise two-piece swimsuit, and with some amusement, Sade could see Raphael struggling to keep his eyes off Tito and then scuttling away.

Tito faced the grown-ups and smiled mischievously.

"Hi, guys."

"Hi, you too," Sade ignored the wet swimsuit and

hugged Tito; Femi slightly squashed between the two women.

"Hi, sis," Lynx's two hands were firmly in his pocket. "To what do we owe this surprise?" His tone suggested the surprise was not particularly welcome.

"If you had your phones on and picked up my calls, it wouldn't be such a surprise." Tito picked on his tone and shivered a tad melodramatically. "It's suddenly become chilly here; I will go in and change. Come Femi, let's go."

Lynx watched her retreating back with a thunderous expression on his face.

"She crashed our holiday, and it's my fault I didn't see her coming! How did she even know where we were?"

"I might have mentioned we were coming here for a break." Sade placated him.

"She called me this morning after you guys left," Teju spoke up from the lounger. "She couldn't get through to either of you. She was at Toulon, and I got Natalie on the phone to tell her where we were."

"Never mind how she came to be here. We are

happy to see her, ain't we?"

"Speak for yourself."

"Aww, my love. I promise you will soon see the upside of this. She will be busy playing the aunt, giving us more time to ourselves."

Lynx looked half convinced. "You don't know her. She loves the party life in St Tropez."

Sade tried to reassure him. "This year is different. She's got a nephew in tow."

They had an early dinner. Tito apologised to Femi after for not having time to pick up a few presents.

"Because you were in such a mad dash to come here from New York?" Lynx asked.

Tito rolled her eyes up in exasperation. "No, I was already in the area."

"How were you in the St Tropez area?"

"I was in Paris. Company business. You could have given me a heads up about your press conference. Now I can't return to New York until it all cools down anyway."

Lynx looked at her disbelievingly. Trust Tito to make everything about herself!

"Pray tell, sis. How are you being punished for my sins?"

"No one can get hold of you, but everyone is calling me. Your friends, my friends, Michelle's friends."

Teju tactfully excused herself from the living room, taking Femi with her.

"Michelle knows already. I told her about my son. She was shocked, but who wasn't at the time?" Lynx said once his son was out of earshot.

"You didn't tell me you spoke to Michelle about our son," Sade said, a bit peeved.

"I am sorry, Sade," Lynx apologised. "It was in the early days. I was not happy keeping my child a secret, and I didn't think it was right that Michelle found out from a third party. But I should have told you I spoke with her."

"Does she think you are with me because of our child?"

"No, Sade, that's not fair. I broke up with her and came to you before I found out about him, remember?"

Tito raised a hand. "Yeah, that I can vouch for!"

"Fine," Sade said. "But can we all get along now, please? We are on a getaway break, after all."

"And I can't think of a better place to have one," Tito added. "Look, Mayowa, I am sorry about turning up here uninvited, but I am here now. I will be out of your hair in three days, tops."

"Alright." Lynx accepted. "Sorry I have been grumpy. I am, of course, happy to see you."

Sade smiled happily and got up. "I will leave you two to catch up. See you soon."

Lynx smiled widely. "Soon, love. Can't wait." His eyes were fixed on her retreating behind.

"Lynx! I am right here." Tito protested.

"Brought it upon your own head, sis." Lynx grinned wickedly.

Tito laughed. "I must confess you two look so happy together."

Lynx leaned back contently. "We are happy together."

"Mum told me about the house. I don't know if it is fair to say things are moving fast or that you are catching up?"

"What do you think? I have an eight-year-old child that I have not been responsible for his feeding, clothing, or housing."

Tito tilted her head to one side. "When you put it like that, it does sound like catching up."

"And if I get to wake up next to Sade every day of my life, I would have lived a very happy life."

Tito jumped excitedly in her seat. "You want to marry her!"

"I will marry her right now if she will have me."

"But?" Tito sensed his hesitation.

"I am a bit scared of asking. What if it ruins everything?"

"What do you mean? You said everything is perfect. Just now."

"The only marriages she's seen are terrible ones. Her parents and aunt Teju's."

"What about our parents? She's met them."

"Only recently. I can't lose her. I don't want to do anything to risk what we have now. And what we have is beautiful. I am happy. And we have got time."

"So, you are going to keep the status quo," Tito

said.

"We are going to keep being happy together. Wherever that may be, work out our routine, spend more time together, and hopefully, the next step should be obvious and not rushed."

*****

They went to Pamelonne beach the next day.

"Not club 55, sorry, sis," Lynx said unapologetically to his sister. "We are going to Les Jumeaux."

"Makes sense," Tito replied. "They are probably the only one with a playground for kids."

Even Teju joined in on the boat ride to Les Jumeaux. Natalie got a supply of motion sickness medicine for her.

"They make you sleepy," Sade warned her.

"Then I shall sleep on the beach," Teju laughed.

Sade wore a two-piece black swimsuit and tied a short sarong of the same colour around her hips. She brought a long kimono cover-up robe in case it got too chilly. Her hair was tied up, exposing her graceful neck. She put on a hat and a pair of dark sunglasses.

She smiled at Lynx as he watched her casually discarding the kimono robe, exposing her flat, lean belly, and sexy hips on long straight legs.

"Are you sure you want to unleash your woman on Les Jumeaux, Lynx?" Tito teased. She looked svelte herself in a pink high-waisted bikini swimsuit and beach skirt.

Lynx wore a white casual long sleeve Henley T-shirt with dark green geometric patterned swim shorts. His shirt was unbuttoned, and his sleeves rolled up.

"Aye," he replied to his sister easily and put on his dark sunglasses for effect. "Les Jumeaux has got nothing on me, sis."

He pulled Sade into his arms, and a laughing Tito took out her phone to take several pictures against the sunrise and the blue Mediterranean Sea.

Femi joined his parents in the photo shoot. Teju and Tito took turns taking more pictures.

Sade found Pamelonne beach vastly different from the Lagos beaches. It was immaculate, and the water was transparent. Les Jumeaux was exclusive, and she felt at ease as they swam and later walked on the sand hand in hand, both oblivious to the many glances their way.

Sade felt a sense of being photographed a few times but was not unduly bothered to her surprise.

"You are used to the camera; that's what it is." Lynx pointed out.

Ahead, Tito and Femi built sandcastles with Declan noticeably close by while Teju sat under the parasol, a drink in hand but already looking like she might doze off at any moment.

Sade looked at her worriedly and said to Lynx, "if all aunt Teju does is sit and lounge throughout this holiday, I worry she might develop a clot in the legs!"

"Let's get our boy and ask Tito to walk the beach with her." Lynx said.

"She is not a pet!" Sade exclaimed, and they both laughed at the association.

Femi walked with his parents, holding on to their hands. He started jumping in between them, giggling as they lifted him.

"Higher!" He screamed each time.

"My arm is going to fall off," Sade warned playfully.

Finally, Lynx lifted Femi and put him on his shoulders, and they continued their stroll.

Tito came to find them.

"Where is aunt Teju?" Sade asked, looking around.

Tito pointed to their parasol some distance away. "That medicine has truly kicked in. She got tired of walking and my ramblings and wanted a quick snooze."

"Let's give her an hour; then all go for lunch," Lynx said.

"Good plan. Meanwhile, I am parched and going for a drink. You know where to find me."

Later over lunch, Tito filled them in on the latest event on the internet and social media.

"You have been spotted in St. Tropez, by the way. The consensus is that you are both ridiculously sexy."

The jury was also out there on whether Lynx had abandoned his child or whether Sade had kept the child away from Lynx, but Tito thought wisely not to divulge that. They would find out soon enough.

Someone had even managed to get hold of the edition of the Queens Grammar term magazine, featuring Sade's interview of Lynx years ago.

"Some of your friends are at Club 55, by the way," Tito said to Lynx. "They have sent me DMs and asked if we care to party with them tomorrow night."

"How did they know you are here?" Lynx lifted a hand. "Silly question. Don't answer that."

"If you all want to party out tomorrow night, I can stay in with Femi." Teju volunteered.

"This is why," Lynx said, "I recommend digital detox. There is a reason our phones are switched off, Tito."

"Sorry, I am not trying to hijack your holiday, Lynx." She pushed her plate to the centre of the table as a red-haired waitress came to clear their table. "Femi, do you want to go to the playground?"

Tito was noticeably quiet on the way back to Le Parcs.

"I thought you guys made up last night," Sade whispered to Lynx.

"We did. There is something on her mind. She's

just figuring out how to say it. I saw her looking at her phone just before we left and screaming silently."

Sade laughed. "No one screams silently, Lynx. That is totally not the point of a scream."

"Oh, but my sister does. She is the only one of her kind. But she does. Watch this space."

True enough, as they walked back into the villa, Tito turned around and faced them.

"Okay, I know I said I wasn't hijacking your holiday, but we have been invited to a private dinner party. On a mega yacht." She paused for effect. "Yemi Makinde's mega yacht. He is arriving in two days. He directly messaged me and left a number to call him back."

"Yemi Makinde, as in the billionaire Makinde?" Teju asked, her eyes wide and round in astonishment.

"Yes, aunt Teju, same one." Tito was bursting with excitement.

Yemi Makinde was one of the wealthiest men in Africa. He was a business genius who had inherited a part of his father's business, just as he graduated from Oxford, and turned it into a multinational conglomerate.

"This association will be good for all of us," Tito gushed. "Sade, maybe you can get to interview him on your show. And Lynx, you are also now a businessman. Me? My firm has been trying to get the Makinde New York account for a while. This is the perfect opportunity. Please, guys."

"My offer still stands," Teju chipped in. "I will look after Femi while you guys party."

"No need, aunt Teju," Lynx said, a frown settling on his handsome face, "do we really want to go partying at the summons of some billionaire kid?"

"Yes, we do! Come on, Lynx," Tito pouted. "You can't speak for everyone." She faced Sade. "I promise, Sade, it will be loads of fun."

Divide and conquer was one of Tito's strategies. Lynx was very much aware of this.

But Sade only shuddered, feeling the hairs on her upper arm standing up.

"Are you cold?" Lynx asked.

She nodded. "And a bit nauseated, to be honest."

"Maybe it was something you ate," Tito said. "I

mean, I felt that tagliatelle tasted a bit funny."

"Maybe," Sade replied. "We can talk about the party later, Tito. Right now, I need a hot drink."

Tito smiled. "At least someone with an open mind."

Lynx rolled his eyes.

*****

"I don't know what it was exactly about what Tito said, but it brought up some terrible memories. It made me feel sick," Sade told Lynx later that night as they settled in bed.

"What memories?" Lynx probed, frowning.

"Of Temilade." Sade's lower lip trembled slightly. "Memories of her writing letters."

Lynx half sat up in bed. "Writing letters? Who was she writing to?"

Sade shook her head uncertainly. "I am not sure."

"You know," Lynx said, drawing her closer. He was worried. "I feel therapy might do some good, my love. You have a lot locked up inside. I am thinking of repressed memories."

"You think I need a shrink?"

"I do. But what do you think?"

"I think I don't want to talk to a stranger."

"Safe space with a professional. I will be there if you want."

"If I do decide to see one, you will be the first to know."

Lynx did not push it. He had sown the seed, and that was some progress.

"In the meantime, you can tell me anything. Anything you remember or anything you feel like talking about."

Sade laughed. "My shrink."

He smiled and kissed the top of her head. "I will be anything you need me to be, my love."

Tito knocked on their door early the next day.

"It just got more complicated. I got a call from New York. Yemi is open to discussing his New York account with me after the party. I have no choice now."

"We need to set some boundary," Lynx muttered under his breath to Sade but said louder, "how......you need to switch off your phone too, Tito."

Sade feeling better in herself, chuckled. "Now I know where Femi gets his tenacity from."

"But have you thought more about it?" Tito asked.

"No, she hasn't, Tito," Lynx replied. "Because she has been busy sleeping, and this party is not occupying her head space."

"How would you know? You are not in her head."

"I would say I know my woman pretty well, Tito."

"I will see you guys at breakfast. I am going for a run. Just keep thinking about it." Tito said and left.

The party invites got delivered after breakfast.

"I presume it is down to you that he knows where to send these. And he invites a child to a yacht party?" Lynx said incredulously to Tito.

"There is a kid's cabin with a nanny on board. It says so on the invite." Tito pointed out.

"It might be considered rude not to acknowledge the invite," Teju said. "It's Yemi Makinde, after all."

Lynx agreed. "You are right. I will call him."

"The invite is quite personalised, isn't it?" Sade said, staring at their names scripted in gold. "Be a bit rude not to accept."

"It adds to your holiday," Tito added, barely suppressing a victory grin. "And takes nothing away from it."

Lynx and Sade left the others behind and spent the morning hand in hand exploring the Musée de l'Annonciade, one of the longest-established modern art galleries in France, where Sade fell in love with some of the works of Matisse, Signac, Seurat, and Dufy.

They strolled down the Ochre streets of the old village after a delicious lunch at the Au Caprice des Deux.

Lynx took her to the parish church, where at the altar was a bust of St Tropez himself. He explained to her that Torpes had been a roman soldier who was beheaded for embracing Christianity. His head was kept in Italy, and his body was placed in a boat and pushed out to sea, where it apparently landed in what was now known as St Tropez.

"The history of our world is filled with blood and tears," Sade said darkly, and Lynx gave her hand a reassuring squeeze.

There were designer fashion shops that stood opposite grocery stores.

Sade contemplated some of the outfits.

"What exactly do you wear to a billionaire dinner party on a mega yacht?"

"I wouldn't worry too much about it," Lynx told her. "Before we left, I heard my meddlesome sister ordering for all of us from several fashion houses in Paris. They will be delivered via La Mole."

Sade paused in her stride.

"Why? Seriously, Lynx. We need to do something about her!"

"You are preaching to the choir. But as you said, what can we do without hurting her feelings?"

Sade gave him a little evil smile. "Don't worry. I will sort it."

"What are you planning now?"

"Nothing much. However, I promise you a front seat. But can I have access to your Joey?"

Joey was Lynx's PA. He had been in and out of Lagos with Lynx's recent disinterest in resuming abode in LA.

"Sure. Dare I ask?"

Sade shook her head and looked at her wristwatch with a frown. "We are nine hours ahead. I will give him a few more hours before calling. He should be up by then."

Femi, Tito, and Teju were visibly thrilled about the upcoming party. Their excitement was infectious.

"You would think I have never hosted epic parties before," Lynx said at dinner that evening.

"Of course, you have. But I have never been this close to closing the deal on a mega account at any of your parties."

"Touché."

However, even Lynx acknowledged that Yemi sounded exceptionally pleasant and charismatic on the phone earlier and was looking forwards to meeting him.

Sade left the dinner table with the excuse that she had a work phone call to make and winked at Lynx, who winked back.

Tito caught the look and said in surprise, "I thought no phone calls were allowed."

Lynx hid a smile behind a cup of tea. "This one is."

Chapter Fifteen

The invitation stipulated a dress code of evening chic for the grown-ups and smart casual for Femi.

Sade insisted everyone had an early night the evening before and got good sleep.

Tito's shipment of cocktail dresses, elegant tops, pants, shirts, blazers, shoes, sandals, and loafers arrived from Paris en route to La Mole in the early afternoon.

An hour later, Joey's entourage of fashion stylists and make-up artists arrived from Paris en route Toulon-Hyeres.

The stylists wasted no time setting up shop and going through all the clothes, footwear, and accessories, setting aside pieces they seemed to consider complementary.

Tito dragged Sade to a side.

"Who are all these people?"

"Your kindred spirits. Any problems?"

"Not really. But…"

To Sade's intense amusement, Tito was politely whisked away before she could say much else.

"You are enjoying this a tad too much, love," Lynx said, watching the look on her face as Tito was taken up the stairs, outfits trailing behind.

"You have no idea," she said smiling, watching another stylist behind him make a beeline for them. "I believe it is your turn, Mr Fernandez…."

Without turning to look, Lynx raised his hands in surrender. "This I am used to, but I am pretty sure Joey has warned them about me."

Sade frowned. "What does that mean?"

"Lynx ne fait que du Lynx," the stylist said with a beaming smile. "Lynx is a stylist nightmare come to life. I am here for you, madame. He is John Paul's today, not mine."

Despite his best attempts, he could not suppress the laughter that eluded his lips. If looks could kill, Sade could have murdered him.

Sade had always been easy to work on, preferring to let the professionals do their job so that she could concentrate on last-minute mental preparation for her interviews.

The Fernandez siblings were somewhat different.

Sade knew Lynx dressed effortlessly and always exuded sex appeal. However, he did not make the job easy for John Paul until he was styled the way he would have done for himself anyway. He had extreme opinions on what he would wear and what he would not be caught dead in, no matter how much they were the in thing.

"Is this all necessary, Sade?" Tito had excused herself to find Sade mid-afternoon. "I mean, I am trying to get the account, not seduce the man!"

"True, there are only very few necessary things in life, Tito," Sade replied offhandedly, slipping a leg through a pair of beautifully cut white trousers. "Certainly not this party we are all going to. Not the amount of clothing you had flown over, yet here we all are."

Tito stared at Sade for a few seconds before bursting into full-blown laughter.

"This is to punish me?"

Sade smiled. "Do you consider pampering

punishment? I suggest you return for some more if we are to make it to this dinner. There is still hair and make-up to do."

Teju and Femi were the ones who probably enjoyed said pampering the most. Femi kept seeking each of his parents out to ask what they thought of each ensemble.

Finally, they were all dressed, groomed, and ready to leave. Sade was picturesque in an ivory viscose satin crepe tux dress with a feather hem that fell just below her knees. Her hair was pulled back from her face in a chignon-type updo hairstyle with a low bun, highlighting her elegant cheekbones and graceful neck, which was adorned with a choker-type gold necklace.

Lynx, looking suave in a dark blazer with a beige button-down shirt underneath, lightly kissed her forehead before they went to join the others waiting in the living room.

"That dress is giving me loads of ideas. Do we have to go to this thing?"

She put a hand to his face and said in a deadpan voice, "yes, we really must."

He chuckled and took her hand in his.

"Shall we go then, my queen?"

*****

Yemi Makinde's yacht was a fascinating white and blue coloured vessel and was simply named 'lost'. Sade found this ominous, given they were on an enormous expanse of water. It had three decks above the waterline.

He received them as soon as they stepped on board. He was a well-mannered and good-looking man, about Lynx's height but a bit heavier. Sade knew he was only six years older than she was.

She was impressed by the warm reception and how he went about making them feel at home on his yacht.

He crouched low to Femi's height and addressed him.

"Ha! The famous Nifemi. It is very nice to meet you. You really are a mini-Lynx, ain't you?"

Femi giggled and shook the billionaire's hand. "Nice to meet you too, Mr Makinde."

Yemi waved a hand. "Oh, do call me uncle Yemi.

My niece and nephew are in the kids' cabin. They are about your age. I am sure you will make good friends."

"You have family on board?" Lynx asked.

"Indeed, I do," he said as he stood up and glanced briefly at Sade. "It's the holiday season. Their parents are joining us tomorrow to spend a couple of days, and then they will all go to London."

"Come on. Let me show you around."

An efficient-looking young man joined them, and Yemi introduced him as his PA, Sesan.

The lower deck housed the crew cabins and the engine room. The beach club was home to a sectional sofa piece, several sunbeds, and a swimming pool and was adjoining a fitness hub with spa, hot tubs, and a gym. The main deck had a sizeable informal lounge with a giant TV screen, a bar, dining, and a galley. There were a few interior staff about. The captain's quarters were next to the bridge. Femi predictably was fascinated by the controls and the crew's uniform.

They ascended through a spiral staircase, next to an elevator, to the upper decks. There were several luxurious en suite cabins, a cosy cinema, and a larger dining room with another bar that opened onto a dance area. They met a doctor and nurse in the medical centre.

Yemi's nephew and niece were in the playroom. Yemi introduced the duo to Femi and the woman who sat with them as Mrs Ajayi, their nanny. Mrs Ajayi was a friendly-looking woman whom Sade guessed to be in her early sixties. She exchanged pleasantries with the group, stared at Sade momentarily, looked away, and promptly asked if Femi wanted to join the other two children in play. Femi looked up at his mother eagerly. She smiled at him and told him to play with his new friends. She missed the nanny gasping before covering her lower face with both hands, but Tito did not.

"Creepy," Tito muttered.

"Did you say something, Tito?" Yemi asked.

Tito gave him a beguiling smile. "Not really. I am just overwhelmed."

The master deck had a helipad, staterooms, a private lounge, dining area, bar, and an office. Yemi's taste in fine art was contemporary, as demonstrated across the several walls of the mega yacht.

"Woo!" Tito whistled. Teju looked around in pleasure.

"Where are your other guests, Yemi?" Lynx asked. So far, they had only seen crew and staff. "Are we too early?"

"No, you are not. It's just us tonight. How about we start with a drink?" He led them to the bar, where one of his staff poured them all drinks. Sade sipped her wine slowly, her face deep in thought.

"Do you do this a lot? Host private little dinner parties on your yacht?" Lynx asked.

"Not a lot," Yemi admitted light-heartedly. "I usually host big parties this time of the year. My yacht is usually in the Mediterranean, so always about these parts. It is fortuitous that you happen to be holidaying here this year. I wanted to meet you unencumbered by the need to play host to a larger group."

Before Lynx could ask his next question, a staff member came to usher them to dinner.

It was a pleasant affair of a mixture of the local French cuisine and, to Teju's delight, Nigerian food as well. She was served a sumptuous meal of amala and ewedu soup with assorted meat types.

"Is that gbegiri soup?" Teju asked in surprise, pointing to a soup dish in the centre of the table.

"Yes, aunt Teju," Yemi replied with a wide grin. "My favourite."

Sade found herself relaxing. "You are an amala and gbegiri kind of bloke?"

"Guilty as charged. It is the key essential requirement of my chefs."

"The chef we saw downstairs is French!" Tito pointed out.

Yemi shrugged. "He learnt his gbegiri recipe rather fast."

"Poor guy." Teju laughed so hard that she had tears in her eyes.

Sade and Lynx opted for the main course of beef wellington while Tito piled her plate with a vegetarian bourguignon.

After dinner, seated in Yemi's private lounge with soft music playing in the background, Lynx casually asked Yemi why his yacht was named 'lost'. He was seated in between Sade and Tito on the large semicircular sofa. Teju sat opposite them.

Yemi looked around and dismissed his staff before responding to Lynx's query.

"It is an acknowledgement of a time in my life," Yemi replied. "I lost my mother years ago. I was schooling in England at the time. My dad became emotionally unavailable. My half-sisters didn't care. I felt lost."

He asked Sade delicately. "Sounds familiar?"

"What?" She blinked several times in some confusion.

"You were orphaned early, no?"

"Yes," Sade replied. This was now common knowledge?

"Have you not found yourself then?" Sade asked him. "If it has been years since?"

"I did, but then I started looking again recently."

"For what?" She asked him.

"For whom." He corrected and briefly closed his eyes before continuing, "for some months now, I had been looking for a Sade Cole."

A sudden silence descended on the room.

"Excuse me?" Lynx broke it; his eyes narrowed to slits.

Yemi waved one hand in the air. "I am sorry about this little charade, but I needed to see and talk to Sade. I couldn't wait anymore. Yes, I have been looking. But I didn't know until recently that she is the Sade Cole I was looking for."

Sade's initial sense of foreboding the moment she stepped foot on the yacht suddenly returned and intensified. Along with it was a clear memory of Temilade writing letters furiously, begging for help, assuring her little sister that help was on the way.

"Why? Why are you looking for her?" Lynx asked, looking from Yemi to Sade, noticing how her face had suddenly become drawn.

"Lynx, let's get our boy and get out of here." She said to him, but her eyes were locked with Yemi's.

"Talk to me, Sade. What's going on?"

"Do you remember when I told you about Temilade writing those letters?" Sade's voice was barely recognisable as she slowly got off the sofa.

"Yes." Lynx got up too. "It was after we returned

from Le Jumeaux. You said it was something Tito said that brought up those memories.”

Tito frowned where she sat, as perplexed as everyone else.

Sade nodded furiously and turned to Lynx. “She was writing to Mr Makinde. She was writing to him.” She pointed angrily to Yemi. “But he wouldn’t help. That’s why…. that’s why she….” Sade buried her face in Lynx’s chest. “She was murdered whilst hustling to put food in my mouth!”

Chapter Sixteen

There were gasps around the room.

"Sade," Lynx held her gently by the shoulder. "Temilade knew this man?"

"Sade," Yemi began walking slowly towards her and said, "you have it wrong. Don't leave. You and I should talk. Please."

"Stay right where you are, Yemi," Lynx warned.

Yemi paused in his stride and put a hand to his forehead. "The math does not add up, does it, Sade? Think about it. Temilade was seventeen. I was nineteen. How could I be the Mr Makinde she was writing to? I was studying in England at the time."

"What do you know of Sade's sister, Yemi?" Lynx asked, the confusion piling on. The evening had suddenly taken the most baffling turn.

"I met her once, a long time ago, the same day I met Sade." He looked at Teju and added. "And aunt Teju."

"Me?" Teju exclaimed.

Yemi nodded. "It was a long time ago. You won't

remember me, but I rarely forget a face."

"I think you need to explain yourself," Lynx told him, his gaze intent on his girlfriend, who now seemed a bit calmer as if she had done the sums too.

"Sade and I are family," Yemi announced, "Sade is my…my family… long lost. I have been looking… My mother and Sade's were sisters."

Teju carefully studied him in bewilderment. "You are Leila's son?"

"Yes, aunt Teju and so, Aisha's nephew."

"Leila?" Lynx asked of Sade. He could feel her trembling and was worried she might have another vasovagal episode. The occasion certainly called for one. He helped her back to the sofa, wiped her sweaty brow, and asked Tito to get her a drink.

Tito quickly did as asked. Teju drew closer to the little group, concern evident on her face for Sade. Yemi briefly went to the bar to get a strong drink and, upon return, sat down opposite them.

Sade glanced at him and, for a split second, saw *her*.

Leila.

Evil, selfish Leila.

"You know this Leila, aunt Teju?" Lynx asked almost in a whisper.

Teju nodded. "She…I was away when she… I met her on a few occasions. She was sophisticated, posh, confident, nothing like Aisha, and not the type you saw in our neighbourhood. She came once with a boy. It was a long time ago."

"That would be me," Yemi interjected. "She took me once to aunt Aisha's. I remember her telling me not to let my father know. I was about ten at the time, but that request only made sense to me recently."

"Sade's never mentioned her, aunt Teju. Not once." Lynx said.

"Leila is difficult to talk about," Teju replied desolately. "Even Aisha did not say much about her sister."

"Why?" Tito asked.

"Because she was a witch," Sade said so quietly that they almost did not hear her.

"No offence taken," Yemi said amicably. "My mother was tough. She grew up in an orphanage. Life taught her to be ruthless in going after what she wanted. She made mistakes along the way."

Lynx scrunched up his brow, remembering something Sade had said about her parents growing up in an orphanage that had niggled at him at the time, and he had thought it was just semantics.

Sade had said they all grew up in the orphanage.

All. Not just her parents. Lynx understood now that she had included Leila as well.

"Who was Temilade writing to then?" Tito wondered out aloud. "The Mr Makinde she was writing to?"

"My father. He never opened her letters."

"So, he didn't know the girls needed help?" Tito deduced. "He didn't know they were orphans?"

Yemi wrinkled his nose. "I am not sure he knew they were fully orphaned. But he at least knew they had lost their father. It was in the same car crash that killed my mom. There were three people in the car, with only one survivor. Sade."

"What! Sade, you were in that accident?" Lynx was horrified.

Sade put her head in her hands. "Yes, I was." She had promised to always tell him the truth. She wished she had not been in the car, but all the wishes in the world could not change what did happen.

"So, what now?" Tito asked no one in particular.

"Sade has to talk to me. I haven't done anything wrong." Yemi said still in his calm voice.

Lynx felt a strong urge to protect Sade from all the unpleasantness, but he knew she had to face these unravelling demons, who had unexpectedly taken the form of Yemi Makinde. A man who was a stranger to them until a couple of hours ago.

But who now revealed himself to be Sade's family.

"I was away, studying in Oxford, at the time of the accident," Yemi was saying. "I came home for the burial, and father thought it was best I returned to school soon after. I found it strange that aunt Aisha did not come for my mother's burial nor to check on how I was coping with my loss. I even resented her for it. I didn't know the person who died alongside my mother was aunt Aisha's husband. My father said he was her chauffeur."

"Why the lie?" Lynx wondered. "What was your father hiding from you?"

"He was hiding the truth."

"Don't," Sade said, almost inaudibly, her lips resuming the trembling.

"You know," Yemi said, a dawning expression on his face. "You know the truth."

A new kind of quietness descended on the room.

"What truth?" Teju asked cautiously.

The silence continued as Yemi stared at Sade.

"What truth?" Lynx asked a bit more forcefully.

"You knew the truth of me when I said I was Leila's son, didn't you?" Yemi's voice was quivering now.

Sade was trembling. "No, you will not do this."

"I have to. The lies have gone on for too long."

"You are my cousin."

"No, I am not."

"Yes, you are," Sade said louder.

"Hold on." Lynx broke in. "What are we missing here? Aisha and Leila were sisters, no?"

"True." Yemi conceded.

"Which makes you two cousins."

"No." Yemi shook his head and pointed an index finger at Sade. "Sade is my mother's… Leila's daughter. Not Aisha's. She is my sister."

"What?" Tito and Teju shouted in unison.

Lynx looked and saw the truth in Sade's eyes. He saw the vulnerability she spent years hiding, the essence of who she was, and understood at that moment how she came to be the person she was- the person who felt the need to keep the rest of humanity at bay.

"How's that even possible?" Teju argued, her voice mildly tremulous. "I was there."

"Were you, though?" Yemi turned slightly to Teju. "Were you there all the time? Did you see Aisha pregnant with Sade?"

Teju squinted her eyes at the distant memory. "No. But she was unwell; she'd lost weight. She went away to her sister's as her husband was incapable of looking after anyone but himself. She took Temilade with her. When Sade was pregnant and ill with Femi, I remember thinking she was just like her… her mother."

Lynx felt a heaviness in his chest. It was unimaginable, the loss, lies and deceit, secrets carried into the grave, and a thirteen-year-old child, alone in the world, carrying all that around with no one to share it with. He put his arm protectively around her shoulders.

"What else do you remember, aunt Teju?" He asked. "You were friends with Aisha."

Teju bit her lower lip hard, drawing a little blood but did not appear to feel the pain. "I was her only friend, but obviously, I wasn't much of a friend now, was I? Aisha mainly kept to herself. Her husband, Danny, on the other hand, was quite popular in the neighbourhood. He was a talented musician, handsome and something of a don Juan. Aisha stayed home looking after their little girl, Temilade. She talked about growing up in an orphanage with her little sister. She was only a couple of years older than Leila. Leila was the beautiful one, and Aisha lived in her shadow all their childhood. Aisha felt lucky to marry Danny. On the other hand, Leila married some rich Ibadan man, but for some reason, the sisters were not so much in each other's lives after, as you would expect, given their childhood when they had only each other. I never understood that, and Aisha only confided in you what she wanted. I learnt to respect that. And I learnt to respect that with Sade too."

"If Leila was away, how did she come to be Sade's biological mother?" Lynx asked, turning to Yemi.

"My mother was never really away," Yemi answered him. "I found out a lot after my father died. To start with, Danny and Leila had been childhood sweethearts."

"You mean Aisha?" Teju interrupted, and Yemi shook his head.

"No, I meant Leila, my mother. Danny and Leila were the original lovers. It was a love triangle as Aisha was also in love with him. This story would have ended with those two lovers marrying, except for my wealthy father coming into the scene. It then became a love rectangle. He was an older man, already married with two little girls of his own. He met and fell in love with Leila very fast. Easy to see why. My mother was very beautiful. He pursued her relentlessly with all he had, and he had a lot. He worshipped the very soil she walked upon. Yes, you could call her a witch. She was also a drug, and he was her addict. I don't know if she ever really loved him for him, but she certainly loved the life he provided for her. He divorced his first wife as quickly as he could to marry her and gave her thirty per cent shares in his company as a wedding present."

"Danny must have been heartbroken," Tito observed.

"He must have been." Yemi readily agreed. "He turned to Aisha in distress, I believe. She might have been his rebound, but maybe on a level, marrying Aisha also meant always being in Leila's life. But my father was not having it. He kept his wife away from those two as much as he could. I truly believe if Aisha had married someone other than Danny, the sisters would have stayed close to the end."

Tito grimaced, thinking Aisha betrayed the sister code but was wise enough to keep this counsel to herself.

"But he didn't keep Danny and Leila away from

each other, did he?" Lynx said.

"No. Love always finds a way. Mother was an exceptional businesswoman and a very crafty one. As a child, I remember my mother always going away a lot on business trips. I was raised mostly by my nanny."

"She was hooking up with Danny?" Teju asked in disbelief.

"He was a musician. He had gigs. My mother was heavily involved in the family business. There was much travelling on both sides. They met frequently. When she got pregnant, she refused to pass the pregnancy as my father's. She told him the truth; said she was sorry and left him. Left us both."

Yemi looked at Teju. "You said Aisha was ill when she was purportedly pregnant with Sade and lost much weight. I think that was depression from her husband impregnating her sister."

"Unbelievable," Tito whispered.

Yemi continued matter-of-factly. "Father found them and threatened Danny's life. He had the resources and would have, mind you, obsessed as he was with my mother. At least both sisters certainly believed he would."

"A deal was made." Lynx surmised.

"Yes, it was Aisha's desperate idea. The sisters went away before the pregnancy became obvious. Aisha returned with the baby as hers. My mother came back home to us."

"Where were they?" Teju asked. "Aisha said she was going to stay with her sister for a while."

"Lies. They left Nigeria. Sade was born in a village in England."

They all turned to Sade at this revelation, but she did not flinch at this information.

"You already know this," Lynx said slowly.

"I do." She said quietly.

Yemi turned to her. "My father passed away recently. I found your birth certificate while searching for what was true and what was not. I found it among my father's files. That's also when I found Temilade's letters."

"Seemed like they carried on with this deceit for years," Lynx said. "Did Leila change her mind again?"

"Indeed, she did. This time with a more elaborate plan. She called me in England to say she was seeing me soon but, I was to keep it between us. That was the last time I spoke to her. The next call was from my father, asking me to come home immediately as my mother had died. This remains the worst day of my life. For all her shortcomings, I loved my mother dearly."

"How," Lynx asked Sade, "did you come to be in the accident?"

"They were stealing me," Sade replied.

"You can't steal what is yours," Yemi argued softly.

"I wasn't hers. They were stealing me from my mother. Taking me away from all I knew, my mother and Temilade."

They were running away with her.

Lynx rubbed her upper arm reassuringly. "So, they were taking you with them. What happened?"

Sade hesitated, her gaze darting to Yemi.

"It's alright," Yemi assured her. "I know it is the tale of how our…my mother died. The accident report has gaps. You are the only one who can fill those gaps.

If you want to."

"Dad woke me up very early that morning," Sade started. "He told me to be very quiet, that he had a surprise for me. I didn't even get to brush my teeth. He took me out of the house. It was still dark outside, and I didn't understand what we were doing out at that God-forsaken hour. But Leila was waiting for us just down the road. Dad asked me to get into her car. He sat in front, and I got in the middle seat at the back. They were both very excited. I asked where we were going, and she said we would finally be a family as we should be. We were headed to the airport and going to live in England, where it was safe. I asked if Temilade and mother were coming with us too."

Sade shook her head slightly at the memory. "Leila could not help herself. She declared herself my birth mother. She, Leila, and not her sister, whom I was calling mother, gave birth to me. She was tired of living a lie, sick and tired of being forced to give me up, of being forced to choose. Her greatest regret was leaving England with me after I was born. I was ripped from her arms when they arrived back in Nigeria. Her sister took away her baby, her sister, whom I was calling mother."

"What happened next?" Yemi asked. It was the first time he learnt about his mother's last moments.

"I asked her to stop the car."

"But she didn't." Yemi deduced.

"No, she didn't. I begged them to take me back to my mother. She said you are now with your mother." Sade broke down in tears. "I didn't mean to do it."

"What did you do?" Lynx asked softly.

Sade covered her face with both hands. "I am so sorry."

Yemi sighed. "It was not your fault."

Lynx held her shaking body firmly, beginning to visualise the tragic event that happened next.

"It doesn't matter now," Yemi was saying. "You were a child. They were the adults. They should have known better."

"I leaned over and pulled the handbrake." Sade sobbed loudly.

"Ha." Tito groaned. "The accident."

"I caused the accident." Sade cried in anguish. "I

killed them both."

"No, you didn't," Lynx told her firmly. "You only wanted them to stop. You had no idea what would happen next. You could have been killed too."

"I had only minor injuries, but they died on arrival at the hospital. The shock was too much for my mother. I never told her what I knew in case it made her more ill. But it didn't matter anyway."

"Your mother didn't will her heart to stop," Lynx said. "Broken heart syndrome is a real thing. I googled it up. It is caused by severe emotional trauma."

"If it makes it easier to accept, my father never truly recovered as well after my mother died," Yemi told her. "He became a different person. The business started suffering. After graduation, I returned as soon as possible to help him."

"What a tragedy," Tito observed with tears in her eyes. "All around for everybody. But Sade…I don't know what to say. I cannot apologise enough for the bitch I was at Queens."

Sade smiled through the tears. "You apologise enough with all your expensive gifts."

Tito sniffled. "They will never be enough. I am so sorry, Sade."

"I know you are sorry." Sade reached out a hand to her. "We are BFFs now, ain't we?"

Tito nodded. "Of course."

Sade wiped her eyes with a tissue and turned to Yemi. "You have suffered too, haven't you? You said no one truly cared for you after Leila died."

"My father was a broken man after she died. I don't know which was more painful for him. He had lost her either way. My older sisters were not very interested in him. They never forgave him for divorcing their mother, and they hated mine. I didn't get along with them in my earlier years."

"Your childhood sounds lonely," Tito said.

Yemi waved a hand half dismissively. "My nanny was great. We are still very close. She is the only one I care to leave in charge of my niece and nephew, and now, Femi, of course."

Tito smiled. "Mrs Ajayi was your nanny?"

"Yes indeed, the very best. She filled the gap created by my mother's partial neglect and my siblings' dislike. She was very protective. I told her about Sade the moment I found out."

"She did give Sade quite the look when we met her," Tito said.

"Oh, God, you are Femi's uncle!" Teju suddenly exclaimed, and Yemi laughed.

"When I told him to call me uncle Yemi, I wasn't kidding."

"But you must have remembered you had cousins. Did you not wonder about them?" Teju asked.

"I didn't know them well," Yemi replied. "Mother didn't take me visiting again, but she occasionally talked about her sister and her daughters. I asked my father about my aunt and cousins much later after my mother died, but he only said they had moved away from Ebute Metta, and he didn't know where they were. The impression he left me, not by anything he said but by his general demeanour, was that they were estranged from him. I don't think he knew Aisha had died too and left Sade and Temilade orphans. I like to believe even he was not that evil. As I said, he was a different man after my mother died."

"In what way?" Sade asked, wondering if a broken heart syndrome had killed him too.

"He became severely depressed, and it affected his memory. He later developed dementia. The business suffered as a result. When I returned from England, he handed over my mother's thirty per cent shares in the company to me. My sisters agreed to become involved in the business only if I sold back to the family my mother's shares, so we all had equal stakes in the company."

"They made you do that?" Tito asked.

"It was a small sacrifice to make," Yemi explained, "to finally make peace with my big sisters. And it was not a bad deal. I got funds to invest in several businesses of my own. I am half Fulani, and I leveraged that identity to make powerful connections with Northern business moguls, many of whom are Fulanis. They saw me as family and nicknamed me the lost son of the caliphate. So, my mother's thirty per cent is today the source of the bulk of my wealth. Do you know where I am going with this?"

"Your wealth is partly Sade's as well," Tito

concluded.

Sade shook her head. "She willed her money to you."

"So I was made to believe, but this is not true."

"What do you mean?" Tito inched forwards.

"After my father died, among other things, I found my mother's will. She willed her wealth equally between Sade and me. It stated clearly, to my son, Yemi Makinde, and my daughter Sade Cole. It could not be more explicit. Her will was never read."

"Your father could not allow it," Teju said sadly.

"No, he couldn't. He feared a part of his company going to Danny Cole's daughter, never mind that my mother had done a lot for the business."

"And this is how you realise Sade is your sister?" Lynx asked.

"Yes, so I searched for more evidence. I found her birth certificate. I found Temilade's unopened letters, asking for help as Aisha had died. Unnecessary. At this point, Sade had inherited lots of money. So, I began looking for my *cousins*. I went to the bungalow in Ebute Metta, but it had been sold. There was no forwarding address. I spoke to the older neighbours and learnt Temilade had died too. Sade left, returned years later, pregnant, and lived with aunt Teju. So, I looked for aunt Teju and found out they both left Ebute Metta at about the same time. I left my number with a few people to call me if they knew how I could find Sade. I got private investigators on the case too. Then one day, I got a call to say the Sade I was looking for was the host of the Cole show on ACE."

Yemi turned his attention fully to Sade. "I was beyond excited the first time I watched your show; tears were streaming down my cheeks, seeing so much of her in you: the mannerism, the grace, the elegance. I knew in my bones you were my mother's daughter. My close advisors were not swayed by such sentiments and insisted on a DNA test."

"DNA test?" Lynx asked.

"I am sorry about this next part. I am not proud of it, but I had to."

"What did you do?" Sade wondered.

"Hair and make-up. I got strands of your hair from ACE. I paid for it."

"Who was it?" Lynx asked. "They are fired."

Yemi pacified him. "It could be anyone, stylist, hairdresser, or even the dressing room cleaner. I just got my people on the job. They could not do a cheek swab for obvious reasons and so settled for as many hair strands as could be retrieved. DNA analysis came back with a high percentage that Sade was my half-sister. The day I received the results was the day of your press conference, and suddenly you were both incommunicado and out of the country."

"How did you find us?" Sade asked him.

"Lynx's private jet was tracked to La Mole, and it was easy to figure out you guys were headed this way. Social media and obviously Tito helped too. I knew she was after my New York account."

"So… Tito was bait?" Lynx concluded with some amusement.

"Not me," Tito gave him a little scowl. "The New York account was."

Yemi laughed. "As I said, my yacht is mostly somewhere around these parts. And I could not wait a moment longer."

His gaze met Sade's again. "At the least, I thought, you had to know me as your cousin, but I wanted you to know I was more. I want to be in your life as I should be. I have not done anything wrong bar yanking a few strands of hair off your head. I am your brother, the only other blood you have left."

"No, you haven't done anything wrong," Sade agreed. "Thank you for looking and for finding me. Thanks for even yanking those strands."

She leaned back into Lynx's chest. "For a long time, I felt like my life was ruined before it had even begun by choices made by others before I was born. I didn't ask to be born into their huge mess."

Lynx kissed her hair. "I, for one, am glad you were born. I only wished you had not suffered so much, but you have been very brave tonight, my love."

"I might go for that therapy, after all, Lynx." Sade unexpectedly announced.

"Oh, I know an excellent therapist," Yemi offered.

"So do I," Lynx countered.

"Mine graduated summa cum laude. From Harvard."

"As did mine from Yale."

"Really, guys?" Tito interjected. "Is now the time to be comparing sizes?"

Yemi chuckled. "Not today, Tito. But he is dating my sister, and he is my nephew's father. I suspect we have much to talk about in times to come."

"Not about me, hopefully." Sade looked from one to the other. "The patriarchy days are over."

"I couldn't agree more," Tito added.

"Of course, love," Lynx said amicably. But he eyed Yemi surreptitiously.

Yemi had nothing on him.

Chapter Seventeen

A *year later....*

"You may now kiss your bride."

Lynx drew his bride's slender waist into his arms under the rose-decked alter and, with the Atlantic Ocean as a backdrop, obeyed the command with fervour. Their guests laughed, cheered, clapped, and even wiped their eyes with tissues.

The wedding was hosted on the main deck of the mega yacht, now renamed *Sade*.

The décor in shades of blue and sea glass green paid homage to the blue ocean around them.

Sade, Tito, Teju, and the bridesmaids, including Anne, whom Sade had reconnected with through Tito, spent the previous night on the yacht. Anne was no nun but a chartered accountant, Sade found to her amusement.

Lynx arrived on board with his parents and Femi that morning. In a reversal of the traditional bride and groom family roles, Tito was the maid of honour and Yemi, Lynx's best man.

"This still doesn't feel right," Yemi had protested at one of the grooms' men fitting. "I shouldn't be your best man but the father of the bride."

"Don't be silly." Lynx had hushed him. "Aunt Teju beats you to that every single time. My sister is the maid of honour and is not moaning about being on the wrong side of the family."

Zuhair Murad designed Sade's wedding dress. It was a champagne-coloured fit and flare silk tuile and sequined gown with a removable overskirt and geometric crystals. She looked regal with her hair styled in a side swept chignon accessorised with a delicate golden hairpin.

Lynx's three-piece black suit was a Saville row piece made by hand and had taken a couple of months to complete. He looked alluring and downright sexy, even more than usual.

The bridesmaids wore smokey blue camisole embroidered midi dresses, while Tito wore the same colour in an A-line scoop neck floor-length chiffon dress with ruffle. Yemi and the groomsmen were in navy blue classic suits.

Anna and Kunle Fernandez, with Teju and Femi, sat in the front row. Femi seemed more interested in the wedding cake than his parents' pledge of undying love. It was a blush pink five-tier pearl-encrusted exquisite wedding cake.

They had a hundred guests on board, including Yemi's two older sisters and their families, Mrs Ajayi, the Fernandez extended family, and Anna's Italian American family. Lynx and Yemi's close friends were also in attendance, as were Tony, Kenny, and Principal Davies. Several bodyguards, including Declan, were unobtrusively about, and so was Lynx's PA, Joey. The ACE network had sole rights to cover the picturesque event.

The new couple turned to their guests after their first kiss. The older Fernandez couple beamed at them, and Femi waved at his parents. Sade and Lynx waved back, laughing.

Their first dance was to the song "heart of this prince", Lynx's version. The song's formal release was the next day, so their guests were hearing it for the first time, and from the excited whisperings around them,

Sade knew it was a hit already. The original song was written for Leila, Sade's biological mother, but today it paid tribute to their own love story. It was Lynx's voice singing to her, telling the tale of young love, enduring over time and distance, a love that always found a way, a true love that never dies.

Sade put her arms around his neck and her head on his chest. She was the luckiest woman in the world.

"I love you." She whispered.

"And I love you." He whispered back.

Interestingly, she had been the one to get down on one knee first. Realising what she was doing, he had immediately gone down on the opposite knee to hers. They had proposed to each other, half laughing and half in tears.

She had told him she could not imagine spending her life with anyone else. He knew her in and out as no one else did. He had been there at her lowest; he had wanted to be with her when she did not have a home and had nothing and no one. He had been beside her at every therapy session as he had promised. He had been there for her from the moment he had met her.

"Yes, I will marry you," he said, feeling his heart might just burst with how much he loved her. She was his life, the very air he breathed.

"I will marry you." She said, sniffling and smiling simultaneously, deliriously happy he had said yes.

After the couple's first dance, two of Lynx's friends took over the musical entertainment, and the dance floor filled up.

Lynx looked around at waiters and waitresses now milling around, at the flow of gorgeous food gracing tables, unending pricey drinks, and the ambience. Yemi had been pleased when they chose his yacht for their wedding. They wanted a cosy affair in Lagos, but some distance from the main city, so they settled on its waters. Lynx's private jet would later land on the helipad to take them to their honeymoon in the Caribbeans.

Kunle and Anna were dancing together, as was Teju and one of Anna's Italian male relatives, who seemed to have taken a shine to her. The maid of honour and the best man were dancing, as were the groomsmen and bridesmaids.

"Your brother has outdone himself."

Sade laughed. "He is still compensating, you know."

Against her protests, Yemi had insisted on giving her a stake in his business, insisting it was her inheritance and the return on its investment. She had tried to dissuade him that she was no businesswoman, but he had only laughed and given her a look. "Try another excuse. You are Leila's daughter."

"I should reassure him we are all right," Sade added, "he doesn't need to keep paying for a past that was not his fault."

"Nah," Lynx feigned disagreement. "Let that billionaire sweat a little bit more."

Sade looked over to where Yemi was dancing cosily with Tito.

"The billionaire is now dancing sensually with your sister."

Lynx did not bother looking. "They are family now. Anything more would be like incest."

"It is ironic, isn't it?" Sade said. "In the end, it was my approval she needed for the account she wanted from him."

"I will never understand why you didn't make her grovel even a little bit for it." Lynx grinned wickedly.

"Ah, what's the point? I'd just be dragging out the inevitable. Talking of which, is there a remote chance I could drag you out of here for a bit without offending our guests?"

His eyes turned dark with desire. He dipped his head to whisper into her ears.

"Really? You are terrible, Mayowa Fernandez." She laughed out loud.

"But you will indulge me, won't you, Sade Cole-Fernandez?"

www.ingramcontent.com/pod-product-compliance
Lightning Source LLC
Chambersburg PA
CBHW031941110726
47902CB00001B/255